A Tree Named Jacob

Charles C. Burgess

PublishAmerica
Baltimore

First printing

All characters appearing in this work are fictitious. Any resemblance to real persons, living or dead, is purely coincidental.

ISBN: 1-4241-7098-2
PUBLISHED BY PUBLISHAMERICA, LLLP
www.publishamerica.com
Baltimore

Printed in the United States of America

A Tree Named Jacob is dedicated to a Tennessee place and its people. Both are physically gone, but their memory lives on in my heart.

Prologue
Aaron Joseph's Reverie

I think I'll just sit down here and rest a spell, take my knife and cut me off a piece of tobacco and put it right here in this old mouth. When I was little, I'd watch my pa take out this same knife and do the same thing and I remember the look of pleasure on his face, wish I could see him do it again just one more time. Told me he'd traded a good coon dog for this Barlow knife, 'bout the only thing I have of his except the Elgin pocket watch, Lord, I almost see *him* when I look at those things. Doggone, hoeing weeds tires me more than doing about anything, at least plowing isn't hard anymore, plowing now with a tractor's easy compared to walking behind those mules, now that was something else. My, think I'll just sit here a minute, it's a mite piece over to the house.

Hmmm, what's this, a little tree, almost stepped on it. It can't be allowed here, no room to grow, and besides, I'll be using this field for corn next year. Lindsey and me took out an apple tree near this very place so I didn't have to plow 'round it… Wonder how in tarnation a maple tree come to grow here anyways, guess probably a strong wind, I've seen wind carry seeds a long ways on their little spinning wings, just like little helicopter planes. They finally spin down to dirt, and the wind keeps spinning them, little at a time, till they're in the ground. Guess the wind was blowing just right for this one.

Its momma was probably the tree near the road; I reckon trees have mommas. My momma said she named that tree after me! Land sakes, don't thoughts get funny when you just sit and rest with nobody 'round? Doves roost in that tree in front of their house; sometimes I've noticed feathers on the ground left over by an owl or hawk.

Wonder if this one will grow tall and round like its mother, or die from wind or lightning. Dry spell could kill it long after I'm gone, or maybe I'll still be here, Lord only knows. Well, like everything else, born, grow up, and someday die, everything's going to die, that's for sure, but maybe it'll leave children to carry on like me and Lissie have with Jacob and Anna.

Thinking of those kids, I'm sure glad they don't live where I had to in the holler. No, sir, no place for a family, coons for neighbors, work, work, work, never play, never having others to play with anyways. What a terrible place to grow up down there. Hadn't been for the water, I suppose we'd still be there, gracious!

Think of all I have, sure don't deserve it all, the house, all this land, full barn, and meat in a freezer instead of hanging in a smokehouse. Our cup is running over, why, even the old sow just gave us twelve more pigs! Wonder why God has given me so much, not sure I deserve it, but I'm grateful.

I think of Jacob when I see this tree, both just starting out, wonder if that's what momma was thinking when she saw the other tree, never thought of it that way, anyways, it's silly to just sit here staring, people think I'm a darn fool, a mind sure gets funny thoughts.

Lord, sure wish Pa could've known Jacob; he's the spiting image of his grandpa. Be fun to let Jacob replant this tree out front of *our* house, I'll have to remember where it is.

Nature's sometimes so cruel, everything wants to survive like the creatures and this little tree, then something happens and they're gone. Sure have seen my share of people dying, the war and all, seems everything in nature wants to keep on living, but it's not meant. Like the Bible says, seasons for everything. I've seen a lot of seasons.

I reckon supper's ready. Better gather up and head in. Lissie, she'll be wondering 'bout me and I don't want her to see me sitting here by myself. She'll think I'm ailing, and if she knew my mind, she'd be sure the heat got to me.

Chapter One
The Beginning

Aaron Joseph Garrett, "AJ" to some, was judged to be a good man; he certainly came from good stock and, like his ancestors, worked hard, was honest, and generally added respect to the family name. When he was young, folks remembered him to be a little shy; more content watching squirrels bark at blackbirds than playing tag or stickball. But certainly no one thought him slow. Fact was, AJ had set down most of them in spelling bees and was known to be quick with numbers when still attending school. Although his formal education was limited, due to circumstances beyond his control, he was looked upon as one with a lot of common sense and others turned to him for council in later years. He was spoken of as being good-natured, mild-mannered, and a quiet and thoughtful person. And before they passed on, some lived to see him grow up from a difficult childhood, go off to war, return with honors, and raise his own family to carry on the Garrett name.

They remembered the young boy who had a keen interest in things of nature, an interest probably caused by the secluded life he lived until he was five or six years old. An inquisitive mind allowed him to recognize plants and animals on sight and a keen ear taught him the sounds of wildlife. Later, to the delight and amusement of his Anna and Jacob, he would mimic calls of a menagerie of wild animals and fowl.

At about age six or seven, he was often seen accompanying Andrew, his father, to the gristmill to get corn ground and there, trying to draw him out, adults coaxed him into some conversation but found the little boy responded with the fewest possible words.

Later, by age ten, after Andrew's accident, others marveled at his maturity, when he would routinely come to the mill by himself, having hitched the mules to the wagon, bringing the corn up the treacherous logging road and down the main pike on to the mill. This was a tedious journey, taking up the greater part of the day, and was a difficult job for someone that young. He would spend little time at the mill making conversation, usually standing aside and listening to the adult discussions of the local news, the forecasted weather, and everyone's potential crop production.

"Well, there's Aaron Joseph. See you got some gunny sacks a corn to be ground, how's your mama and papa?"

"They's okay, Pa's getting 'round better and Ma's fine, I got eight bags here, but first Pa wants to know if you could take your share from the next batch, we're running a little low right now, but we got more to shuck in the crib when we kin get to it."

"'Course, Aaron Joseph, a Garrett's word is good."

"And Pa wants to know if you have any tobacco twists left, said if you can spare, he'll make it right later."

Without hesitation and returning from a backroom, just as the flowing meal filled the sacks, the owner tossed him a twist of tobacco saying, "Give him this, tell him he owes me a nickel sometime," and he grinned.

"Much obliged, he'll pay, he's better, like I said, guess I'd better be getting back now," and with that he loaded the corn meal, lifted the reins to the mules, and with clicking sounds from his mouth commanded, "Giddy up," and the docile animals lumbered forward. The wagon turned and headed down the road back towards home.

Ever since they had married, Andrew and Sarah, AJ's father and mother, had lived in the holler not far from the Obey River. The twenty-some acres and humble dwelling, barn, storm cellar, and crib, had belonged to the Garrett family perhaps forever, or at least longer than anyone could remember. In the old house, AJ was born, as was his sister, Cordelia, who caught pneumonia and died in infancy. Folks talk of her little body being brought up the steep logging road in a pine box that had been gently placed on the wagon's bed. Upon reaching the top of the hill, it was respectfully carried from the wagon and loaded into a hearse, that proceeded to the church cemetery, where it was buried. Later, Andrew and Sarah placed a small sandstone marker at the graveside, on which a local mason had chiseled *BABY CORDELIA GARRETT*. Sarah visited the site often and grieved and grieved over that little grave.

Not long after the baby's death, Andrew had his accident. Afterwards, he related that he was attempting to remove a tree at the edge of the field, a large tree that blocked any attempt to enlarge the planting area, so he decided to cut it down and snake it to the side. Halfway through its bulky trunk, it prematurely cracked and came quickly down, but with a portion of it, splintered, still attached to the trunk. Trying to pull it loose from the lower side, he wrapped a heavy chain around it and attached the chain to the mules. Something spooked the mules, and they pulled with an unexpected start, causing the trunk to come loose and roll towards Andrew, and before he could back out of the way, his body became trapped under the greater part of the tree's weight. He lay there unable to get free for over an hour. A leg was broken and time would also reveal permanent damage to his spine. AJ found his father in this helpless state when he brought him a cool bucket of drinking water sent by Sarah.

"Lord, Pa! You're hurt, are you able to get up?" AJ asked with alarm.

"I'll be okay, settle down, go fetch your ma, tell her she might bring a shovel, you unhitch Sadie and Sallie and take them back to the barn when you get Ma. I'll be fine, but my leg's hurt and something's wrong in my chest, it's throbbing and feels like something broke."

With that, AJ ran quickly as told, and returned with Sarah, shovel in hand, and she began to dig Andrew out. Finally enough dirt was removed below to free him from underneath the tree. Now growing pale, he commenced to experience breathing difficulty.

"Aaron Joseph, your pa's hurting bad and we'll be in need of help to get him to the clinic." Sarah wiped perspiration from Andrew's head, and continued, "Go see if Cletus Skaggs is home, tell him what's happened, tell him we need him to come, hurry up now!"

The sun was near setting when AJ and Cletus got back and by now Andrew was becoming faint. They found a wide plank in the barn and proceeded to roll Andrew onto it. By this time Sadie and Sallie had been hitched to the old wagon, and the three lifted a hurting Andrew to the wagon's bed and slowly moved up the bumpy and rutted lumber road.

Months passed before Andrew's leg healed enough to allow him to hobble around. The Skaggs family had insisted he stay at their home so they put him up, knowing that Sarah and AJ would have their hands full harvesting their meager crops. Mary Skaggs cared for Andrew—she had known him since they were young schoolmates—until he was well enough to return home. Watching him, she knew he would never be whole, and felt sorry for both him and Sarah. The nature of a broken leg, and a crushed knee, both now supported by a metal brace, caused him to walk stiff-legged with a severe limp, and combined with an injured back, it caused his gait to be slow and painful.

Sometimes Sarah would watch from the window as a hurting Andrew limped to the barn, and her tears gave way to deeper feelings within her heart. One false step, she thought, as many had pondered before and after her, and their lives were changed forever, just seemed so unnecessary and unfair. Why? Andrew was such a good man and provider.

Thereafter, on better days, Andrew was able to feed the livestock and do other minor work in the garden but he had to rest often. His body had been generally weakened and when winter came, he developed a bad cough and later came down with a high fever that drove him to what would become his deathbed.

Within a week, late at night, Sarah awoke to Andrew's moans; he asked her if baby Cordelia was all right, and had she seen his mother, who had passed away many years before. Realizing he was delirious from fever, and had taken a bad turn for the worse, she called AJ, directing him to go to the Skaggses and see if they could reach Dr. Qualls. "Tell Cletus your pa has gotten bad, and is coughing up blood."

Immediately, with lantern in hand, AJ stumbled up the poorly lit logging road on foot, hardly able to see the dirt under his feet. He heard strange night sounds coming from the upper branches of the trees, and a hoot owl's screech brought goose bumps to the back of his neck. These sounds of the dark woods were terrifying even when he heard them from the safety of the house, but now they were overhead and close, but they had to be ignored.

Over three hours passed, it was two a.m. before AJ, Dr. Qualls, and Cletus returned to find Sarah sitting on the edge of the bed and crying. Alone, she had lost her thirty-two-year-old husband, who died not knowing she was present. Although Andrew had passed before help arrived, it's unlikely they could have made a difference. Dr. Qualls report said that Andrew had died of pneumonia and heart failure brought on by a weakened body.

Most all in the community were present for Andrew's burial at the little church and they tried their best to comfort a confused, shocked Sarah and her young son.

The gathering watched as the husband and father was lowered into the earth next to his baby daughter Cordelia. The widow did not want to leave, but ultimately, Sarah was urged from the graveside and AJ looked back, watching the shoveling of dirt into the grave. Later, they accepted a ride to the Skaggs home and, upon turning down a request to spend a few nights, proceeded over the hill with Sarah's arm draped over AJ's shoulder.

Aaron Joseph Garrett, now twelve years of age, ended his formal education but his appetite for learning never stopped. Somehow, he found the time to read all the books and magazines offered to him by townspeople, and he pored over the Garrett family Bible, adding to its already aged pages. For now, fate required him to shoulder the heavier work of running the small farm along with his mother, Sarah.

Chapter Two
Difficult Times

He never forgot the hardships faced during the weeks of his pa's partial recovery in the Skaggs home, and those hardships only increased after Andrew returned home. Now, with his passing, the burdens were almost unbearable for one so young, but his mother needed him desperately for she had no one else.

Nights, when he was too tired to fall asleep, he would lie awake and wonder about work that had to be done the next day, what he would face, and would he be able to do it all by himself. He'd think of David of the Bible, the young Lincoln, and Daniel Boone and the heroics of local Alvin York, but his thoughts would eventually come back to the need for plowing the truck garden, then the big field, potatoes and corn to be planted, and these needs took control of his thoughts. Fortunately a member of the Skaggs family or someone from the church would drop by with a mess of something they'd harvested from their garden, and lend a hand helping him with a chore. Their help was desperately needed and appreciated.

Word got around about the plight of Sarah and AJ in little meetings usually held at the church and baskets of food would arrive unexpectedly during the week, and once, a group of men came by and spent the entire day performing work known to be necessary that time of year. Their kindness shown during this time would never be forgotten and one day he would recall and tell his children about the help they had received. Somehow they got by, one day following another, but the work seemingly never ended.

Some evenings, years later, with Anna and Jacob at his side on the front porch, he'd recall and tell them of the dark, scary nights in the holler, just he and their grandmother Sarah, and the fearful night sounds.

"Why, one night we were both getting ready for bed when your grandmother said to me, 'Aaron Joseph, shhh, stay still for a minute, do you see that mouse sticking its head through that little hole in the wall, over there, next to the Sears Roebuck ad?'"

AJ explained that their walls in the holler house had been wallpapered with newspapers stuck to the wall with flour paste. There was a John Deere ad, and one from Sears Roebuck, another from Montgomery Ward and others all around the room. Over time they were memorized from constant reading. Sarah reckoned that the mouse had eaten a hole through the wall, being attracted by the paste.

"I see it, Ma. What you want me to do?"

"Get me the broom; I'll take care of this little devil."

"Your grandmother whaled the tar out of that mouse,

only it wasn't a mouse. Turned out, it was a big hog snake that slithered to the floor that we killed with a hoe. Lord, it scared us." Anna and Jacob's eyes grew large as their minds tried to envision such a sight.

There was the time the fox got to their five chickens, killed them all, and the time the raccoon got in the corncrib and became mean when AJ opened the door to get some feed for the livestock, and how he had placed a blacksnake in the crib to keep the mice at bay.

And the time a stranger came out of the woods and disappeared up the logging road only to be shortly followed by two armed law officers asking them if a stranger had passed by and explaining that he had been operating a liquor still over on the vacant Ledbetter farm. Locals often wondered what would finally happen to the farm since Ezra Ledbetter had recently joined his deceased wife, Mary, and they had no heirs. Now the county might be more encouraged to do something about the property.

Neither Sarah nor AJ had ever seen a law officer in the holler before this incident and the officers departed as hurriedly as they came. No one ever knew if they caught the scared runner but it made for choice speculation months thereafter. At least one spokesman, himself noted for excessive drinking, volunteered he might have known the renegade from past dealings, and this confession delighted listeners who credited him as authoritative.

Aaron Joseph could relate stories past bedtime and anxious ears listened to every word, tales they would someday pass on to theirs.

Had Aaron Joseph foreseen the future, he would have seen a loving wife and children in a happy setting, and that anticipation and hope would have made life much easier for him to bear this time in his life.

That first winter without Andrew was particularly hard but fortunately the previous summer's crops had been harvested and Sarah had canned beans and corn and blackberries that she had made into jam. Still, the food supply had to be rationed for themselves and the livestock as well, and on many days, the two decided that a bowl of mush with a little milk would be enough, with maybe a baked sweet potato prepared in the ashes of the fireplace. He would remember the treat of crumbling cornbread in a glass of milk and spooning it out and other times, rewarding themselves, they spread a little jam on the cornbread for sweetness. Times could have been a lot worse, they agreed.

Just gathering enough wood to fuel the fireplace and keeping the cow and mules fed seemed enough challenge when the snow started to fall. The nights were long and darkness came on quickly, and having only a meager supply of coal oil for their only lamp, that supply also had to be rationed for emergencies. Often Sarah and AJ sat and talked by the flickering light given out by the fireplace and planned the next day, the next week, and the oncoming summer. Sarah realized, however, that her son was growing up and shouldn't be expected to dedicate his life to her.

Chapter Three
The Coming of the Dam

It seemed improbable that they had endured the first full year, then another, and two others, and with their passing, the chores seemed to grow easier as work became more routine in nature. Physically stronger, AJ was going on sixteen now, near six feet tall, and, thanks to his mother, whom he resembled, struck a rather handsome figure. Four years of hard work had hardened him and he was taking on the looks of a grown man. Life had been difficult but they had worked hard and had gotten by, surprising many in the community. In fact, not only had they survived, but they had also managed to accumulate several hundred dollars now secreted away in a mason jar in the barn. The small, but very fertile river bottom farm, along with favorable weather, had provided exceptional yields, and the limited acreage allowed quick harvests, giving AJ the opportunity to hire out and help others with their crops.

The year was 1939 and changes were in the making that would alter not only the lives of Sarah and AJ, but, in a broader sense, the lives of the whole world for that matter. Somehow though, the affairs of the holler took precedence over Hitler's invasion of Poland; not saying there was a lack of interest in the worldly affairs, it was just hard for them to relate to problems that far away. And had it not been for Cordell Hull, a local boy and the Country's Secretary of State, the problems in Europe would have totally escaped the laid-back discussions that took place Saturday mornings on the courthouse square.

It was credited to listening to these discussions that AJ was able to keep abreast of all matters of importance, and he would return home full of this latest news and share it with his mother. Since their battery-powered radio, listened to sparingly anyway, had long expired, these Saturday visits became a vital means of communication.

It was on a Saturday trip to town, to pick up a new plow blade, when he came upon such a gathering. Basil Strode, looking a little bit surprised, purged his mouth of tobacco juice, wiped his lip and greeted him.

"Look who's here, Aaron Joseph Garrett, where you been so long, boy, how's your Momma Sarah doing?"

"She's just fine, thanks," AJ answered, "been busy plowing this past week, 'bout got it done, broke my plow blade on a doggone rock, seems like there's always something, like Sallie, one of our mules, stumbled yesterday, scared me to death, afraid it'd come up lame, but the tough thing got right up good as new."

"Well, tha's good, say, AJ, has anyone from the government been down to your place?" he inquired as he looked upward, once again eliminating the tobacco juice, and looking in askance toward AJ with squinting eyes.

This question got AJ's complete attention; he knew that government men usually brought trouble, remembering the officers chasing the moonshiner, and he feared he had done something to offend. He replied, "Haven't seen a soul down at our place," continuing with a half smile, "maybe road down's too steep for them. Was someone asking for me or my momma?"

Recognizing he had caused concern, Basil stated he'd heard nothing about them by name, but he went on, "No, jus' heard some men been coming 'round talking to people in the lower parts, heard they's laying plans for that dam to be built, they's a needing the ground, and I guess askin' people to move out, some gettin' real riled up. Might be watching for 'em, and I'll sure let you know if I hear anything more."

AJ returned and related his conversation with Basil to Sarah, starting a great deal of speculation as rumors of the Obey River being dammed up had been going around for ages; something about making cheap "tricity," like they used in town, available for everyone

Shortly thereafter, walking back from the Skaggs farm, a car slowed down near AJ and a man wearing a suit and tie, and official looking, looked over the top of his glasses and asked, "Boy, do you know where the Garrett place is. Been told its somewhere around here."

"I'm a Garrett," AJ replied, "farm's down there a piece," pointing to the small clearing and logging road that went over the hill and disappeared into the woods.

"Sarah A. Garrett live there?" he inquired.

"She's my ma," AJ replied, as he studied the stranger.

"I need to see her, need to talk to her about a business matter," he stated, again looking over the top of his glasses.

AJ, assessing the man as trustworthy, suggested, "Welcome to walk down with me, but I wouldn't try to drive it though, its awful rough going."

With that, the man pulled his automobile off to the side of the road, stopped the engine, and got out. The two proceeded down the logging road, with AJ studying the man's portly stature and labored gait, guessing that the stranger was unaccustomed to such walks. "I think walking downhill's harder than going uphill," AJ remarked, an attempt to be friendly.

"Think it might be," the man replied, panting as he spoke, and relief showed on his face when they finally came to the farm clearing. They approached Sarah, who was returning to the house from the barn.

"Mrs. Garrett," the stranger said, clearing his throat, "my name's Claude Browning, I'm from Nashville, I'm with the Tennessee Valley Authority." He extracted a little card from his shirt pocket and handed it to her.

"Yes," Sarah quickly responded with some concern in her voice, "what's wrong?"

"Nothing's wrong, ma'am," Browning replied, "can we sit down just a minute, that's really some walk down here and its made me a little winded."

"Could I get you a dipper of water?" Sarah offered.

"No, ma'am, much obliged, I'm not thirsty," Browning responded, a decision probably influenced by observing the communal bucket.

"Well, what's your business, Mr. Browning?" Sarah inquired, as she studied his face.

"Mrs. Garrett, we're about to start something down in these parts, maybe you've heard of it, it's a project that the federal government is undertaking with the State of Tennessee. We're going to build a dam and dam up the Obey River. Now when we do, this place of yours is going to be covered with a lot of water and every other low place around here. Water's going to fill this whole valley and folks are going to be asked to move out before the water backs up, probably all happen, we estimate, within four years."

"Land sakes, we can't move, we've no place to go, and this place is our home, only place we got. Why, this land's been in my late husband's family since the government gave it over to Archibald Garrett in 1706, it's all we got and we can't leave. Garrett people are buried up there on the rise." Sarah, obviously getting upset, pointed to the distance at a row of tombstones.

AJ studied his mother's eyes and saw they were welling up with tears, and pleaded, "Best we drop it here, Mr. Browning, momma's a getting worked up."

Browning sensed the growing tension and calmly cautioned, "We're not here to hurt anyone, we're going to make life better and easier for everybody but some have to give for the good of all. We're bringing electricity here for everyone to use. Now the government will be fair with you, pay a good price for your property, even help you find something else, and, if need be, help you move. Don't want hard feelings but sooner or later we'll need all this property around here, that's the law. Now I suggest you talk it over with the folks in town and I'll be back next month when you've had time to consider, then we'll sit down and come up with a fair settlement and I'll know more about the timing, I'll help you all I can."

Leaving them with stunned looks on their faces, Browning bid them a good day and hiked back up the logging road.

Not long afterwards he was back, and by then, everyone owning land in the lower parts had been contacted. Little else was now discussed in the courthouse bench forums.

Chapter Four
The Exodus

Sarah accepted that there would be no recourse and no way to resist. The flood was coming and no one could stop it. Lawyers, some from faraway places, advised their clients to resign themselves and negotiate their best settlement, but because Sarah couldn't afford such advice, and also feeling that she could do her own talking, she sat down with Browning, and two other men, at the courthouse.

He told her that workers would be arriving, some from as far away as Nashville, and they would soon begin to clear cut timber throughout the whole valley and later others would arrive and commence removing houses, barns, and other outbuildings.

Numerous papers were placed before Sarah, who sat stoically at a big rectangular table facing Browning, along with Mrs. Pendergrass, a local witness, and two men from the State Capital, Nashville. Each page in the fearful stack was written in language foreign to her and required tedious interpretation. Mostly, she just nodded as if to understand because most of the legal jargon was beyond her comprehension. AJ sat to the side trying to listen and learn but was perplexed by all the talk about metes and bounds, fee simple estate, and strange words such as whereas, thereto, and talks of deeds requiring some sort of warranty.

Two fifty an acre, that's what they would pay, and Sarah and AJ would have six months to move with a possible six months' extension if they needed more time, but they would have to apply for the extension in writing by a certain date. Payment would be made within thirty days, unfortunately no assistance with the move of personal belongings, and if formally requested in writing, they could have possession of the lumber from the torn-down house and outbuildings but it had to be moved out by the final deadline. All flowed forth legal sounding and precise.

"Yes, Mrs. Garrett, the government will relocate those buried on the property. We can't be responsible for condition of the remains. No, Mrs. Garrett, no compensation for any growing crops, the Government's very strict on what we can do and can't do, and if you don't have any other questions," Browning looked at Sarah, then glanced over at AJ, "we'll get on with it, we've got four more people coming in today."

Sarah, sensing this was a little different attitude than the one she experienced at her home, shook her head and replied, "Reckon won't do no good," and commenced to sign the documents while feeling she was breaking a trust bequeathed to her by Andrew and his ancestors.

Once again the tears welled up in her eyes and AJ noticed.

Only a few weeks after the meeting, trees began to fall on a distant ridge and their felling opened up vistas heretofore unseen. "Look, there's Cletus's barn and you can see where the pike makes its turn heading to town," Sarah would exclaim in amazement.

Massive oak trees many thought to be over a hundred years old, some even serving as survey markers, many beautiful bluish gray-bark beech trees, Andrew's favorite tree, and the plentiful shag bark hickories, all came crashing to the earth, where most would be left to decay.

Wildlife commenced its exodus as the deer, the gray squirrel, the raccoon, and fox were also losing their ancestral homes. Farmhouses, some dating to the 1800s, that had been reliable shelter to several generations, barns, cribs, all would be emptied of their humble personal items and then reduced to rubble, and become only memories.

Great sadness filled the valley years before the water, water that mixed with the tears, and water that would eventually wash away the memories. A history of the lake would later record, almost as a footnote, *the water completely covered the old Garrett place*, without regard to the generations that went before.

Three weeks later, Sarah opened the long brown envelope and studied the check left in their mailbox up on the pike: *PAY TO THE ORDER OF: Sarah A. Garrett, $5,500.00*, which she later signed and handed over to the bank for safekeeping, a little piece of paper, she thought, in exchange for the house, the land, the barn and the pretty woods and memories passed down for generations. Although she sensed it being a lot of money, many times more than she had ever seen or expected to have in her hands, it seemed such an unfair exchange, while actually it was a rather generous settlement.

They'd be moving to the old Ledbetter place, twice the acreage they had in the holler, and the fields were much more level. AJ had hunted on this land and he always marveled at how different the terrain was considering its closeness to the bottomlands. Sarah had driven a good bargain with the county, and would only owe them three thousand dollars, that she felt able to handle. The taxes would be higher, probably up to thirty-five dollars a year, but they'd make it.

Fortunately, the Ledbetter property was in reasonably good shape. While Ezra had not personally farmed his land, he had leased it out to others and they had kept the fields from becoming overgrown with weeds and sassafras. This was the fear with any unused vacant land; fear that the weeds and the stubborn sassafras would reclaim it.

The barn was larger than the one in the holler and it was sturdy, as was the ancient farmhouse. Both would require the securing of a few boards here and there, and there was a chicken house needing a new roof, an adequately sized smokehouse in good shape, and a corncrib. A small slope behind the farmhouse fell off just enough to provide the location of a storm cellar dug into the side of the hill. In severe weather it served as a safe place, and all other times, a place for the storage of canned goods. Novel to the farm was a small water house that had been built to cover the good producing well.

Just below the barn, in a low area in the adjoining field, Ledbetter had allowed his pigs to wallow and compact the soil. Eventually a small pond had formed, filled by the rains, and the water made an excellent watering hole for the livestock, and later, AJ, with the help of resource people, would introduce fish to the pond.

And sometime in the past a gentle breeze had carried a red maple tree seed to the field in front of the house, where, finding fertile soil, and unnoticed by human eyes, it would sprout and grow in height and mark the human changes, and a new cycle would begin for it and for the caretakers of the land that God had loaned them. Sarah spotted the well-formed tree, saw that it was making a new beginning, and thought, *I think I'll call that tree Aaron Joseph, he's getting grown up too,* and she smiled at the thought.

Trip after trip they carried their personal belongings to slowly transform this place into their home. Up came the beds, the dresser, the kitchen table and chairs, and the utensils, back and forth, back and forth, and finally barn items began to appear. Then come the canned goods, placed in the storm cellar, and the salted meats from the smokehouse were hung in their new places. It took over three weeks to move it all but they had beaten their tight deadline with time to spare because they had found a new place so quickly.

Sarah sighed, "God's watching over us, Aaron Joseph, I reckon we'll do just fine, but I'm going to miss home."

One last walk around the old place, the walk to the barn, where they reclaimed the mason jar with its money, and Sarah gave a running account, possibly her way of making sure the memories were secure in her own mind,

"Over there, that's where the copperhead snake was by the woodpile, this place's where we planted the beans that did right well, over there, that's where you fell that time and hurt your leg, oh me, up there's the empty graves, here's where I had to sit down and rest when I was carrying you, almost birthed you right here, they had to carry me inside, Lord, Aaron Joseph, I've got to leave, can't stand it anymore… And there's where your daddy had his accident. Lord, Lord, help us," and they headed up the logging road the last time, only occasionally looking back.

AJ thought, *This is the way I felt when I had to leave Pa's funeral,* and although he would return to the old place over the hill from time to time, to see what work had been accomplished, and on one such trip observing that the buildings had been removed, he never told his mother. Sarah never returned and only a few times inquired about the progress, as her way of avoiding the emotional pain.

-§-

Chapter Five
A New Beginning

Fortunately the mason jar money was enough to allow the purchase of seeds for crops the oncoming season. Now, with favorable weather, they anticipated the potential harvest exceeding that realized in the bottomland.

They gradually become accustomed to interacting with their neighbors along the pike, and in time were able to accept the sound of vehicles passing by on their way to town. Standing on the road, without actually seeing the vehicles, they could hear the singing tires from miles away heralding a soon arrival; and AJ would look down the road in anticipation and guess as to the type of vehicle.

There was the rolling store, it came by twice a week, carrying items not locally grown such as coffee and sugar, a daily bread truck, the Coca Cola truck, and the Esso fuel truck, all passed and waved or honked horns in passing. Sometimes, if they happened to be in the front part of their property, and the timing was right, they would encounter the mailman making his daily run, and he would offer a ride into town, seemingly pleased to have the company, and as a bonus, he could be counted on for the current news.

AJ particularly welcomed the stopping of the rolling store where he was able to exchange three or six eggs, depending, or a bucket of blackberries, for any number of "store-bought" items that had been unavailable to them in the holler. Occasionally he would surprise Sarah by presenting her with a new bonnet or apron, and the seemingly ever-present sadness would leave her face albeit for a moment.

There were more pleasantries, the pitch-in suppers, church services every Sunday, sometimes featuring a traveling evangelist passing through, and of course the holiday celebrations, but no special event could ever really replace the weekly church service for its spiritual and social contribution to the community.

"Aaron Joseph, be sure and tell Sarah about the pie supper we're having after church next Sunday," Preacher John Sewell cautioned as they passed in town earlier in the week. "If she'd bring one of her blackberry pies, it'd fetch a pretty penny, and the church could use the money. Gracious, her pies are good, my mouth waters thinking about it, I might buy it, what'd you think about that?"

Now AJ knew that competing for an individual's pie was a very personal act, and he was also aware of Sewell's bachelorhood, but he liked the man, and didn't hesitate, "That'd be fine with me, Brother Sewell."

Many years later, while listening to a familiar hymn on a gospel radio station, AJ remembered details of that particular church service and the pie supper that followed. He remembered how Brother Sewell manipulated, and gained advantage in the bidding process to get Sarah's pie, only to see victory snatched from him.

"That pie will be mine, I'm bidding seventy-two cents," Sewell boasted in triumph, having doubled the previous bid. He started his march toward the raised platform to claim the spoils and sported a broad grin.

"Whoa, not so fast, I don't think so, I'm bidding ninety-five cents for that pie and the cook has to eat it with me," an unexpected bid came from a man sitting in the rear.

Sarah, flabbergasted and embarrassed, placed her hand over her mouth to hide the smile. AJ watched and could not remember the last time he had seen happiness in her eyes, but who was this stranger, she wondered, certainly he was not from the area.

Earlier two men had arrived in an ancient vehicle and entered the church explaining that they were workers on the dam. After qualifying talk, to confirm their salvation status, they were welcomed with many handshakes and urged to stay and enjoy the service. One of the two, the bid winner, Lindsey Stone, would relate to Sarah as they were eating that he had been hired as foreman to oversee the cutting of timber, was boarding with some people some thirty miles down the pike, that he was from a town in central Tennessee, not far out of Nashville, had lost his first wife to tuberculosis, and had a six-year-old daughter, Kathryn, back home with the grandparents.

He fascinated her with the story that an ancestor of his, Samuel, might have been one of the earlier settlers in this very area and that had influenced his acceptance of the job.

Sarah, in turn, explained how she had lost her man through an accident and that she and her son, AJ, were victims of the oncoming flood but had successfully relocated. She felt a little resentment that Lindsey Stone was party to hardships they had faced, but kept this in her heart, recognizing that here was probably a decent man.

In studying him, Sarah remembered reading long ago about Irving's Ichabod Crane character in the writer's story *The Legend of Sleepy Hollow*, and with the hint of a smile, she compared this character to Lindsey Stone. But Lindsey, she later thought, didn't fit the role of a schoolteacher and was definitely not awkward in manner. They enjoyed each other's company, and would meet again, to the great discouragement of Brother Sewell.

Aside from this event, though, AJ would remember his mother as the way she was so puritanical. She dressed the image in her ankle-length dresses, colored gray, or brown, and seemingly the dresses had never been new. She accessorized her dress with laced black shoes and an old black purse and AJ would later wonder when and where she had acquired them. The shoes, run down, were her only pair, for they were the same she wore on weekdays as she fed the chickens, milked the cow, or performed unending other labors.

Her premature graying hair—she was now in her late thirties—was pulled back into a bun, commonly seen on older women, or seen on those of a certain religious inclination, and the bun had a short, curved brown-speckled comb plunged through its center. He remembered her long hair and the many times he had watched as she lowered her head, tossed her hair forward, and began to comb until it glistened. The hair almost touched the floor before she began to create the bun.

But despite her attire, his mother's natural beauty, due to her fair skin and fawn-like eyes, glowed in a way AJ hadn't seen since his father died. Ultimately Lindsey Stone would add great richness to his mother's life.

Two other powerful memories remain about that humble frame church. First, there were the songs of course, and second, the sincerity of those present. This sincerity was projected by expressions on sun-browned, wrinkled faces and further demonstrated when they uttered "amen" now and then, emphasizing approval of what Brother Sewell said.

The music AJ heard today triggered all those recollections and he saw the gathering in his mind's eye, causing him to smile; it was pleasant to see them all again.

The building was just a large rectangular room containing movable tables and a potbellied wood-burning stove. The stove, centrally located in the room, served to separate younger from older students filling the room on weekdays. AJ remembered when he had attended school before the death of his father, and the memories were pleasant. The church service, and the pie supper, was held on a summer Sunday, so the stove now sat still and cold. The structure itself, AJ knew, had been erected to satisfy the need for a schoolhouse, and served that primary need on weekdays, but it became a holy place on Sundays with no consideration given to separation of church and state.

He remembered the desk in the front of the room that was used by his first grade teacher, who also taught grades two through eight. A blackboard was prominent on the wall behind the teacher's desk, but otherwise, the walls were plain and undecorated. The building was Spartan simple, and did not fit the romanticized look often seen on Christmas cards. No spire, no belfry, no stately cross was there to hint of its Sunday use.

In this rectangular structure, AJ had labored over his ABC's, basic arithmetic, and learned to spell his first words from his reader, and here, on Sundays, he heard about God and Jesus and the Holy Ghost and Satan and hell's fire. He heard about those who needed some sort of help, the weather, a neighbor who had an accident at the mill, and what crops were growing well this season.

Preacher Sewell was fundamentalist in belief and his message thundered that theme. The theme was often repeated, sin, *without* forgiveness, first from God and second, from your neighbor, and you were doomed to hell's fire, but abide by the Golden Rule and the Ten Commandments, and there was some hope. Avoid temptation! AJ heard the whispers about certain backsliders and noted that a lot of prayers were directed their way.

He saw a fearful vision that the preacher described, a vision strengthened by looking at the adult faces, some watery eyed when song and sermon filled the room. He thought, more than anything, the faces displayed hope, and he saw a special contentment when they sang about the sweet by and by, and the land where they'd never grow old. Peace seemed to come on their faces when songs that reminded them of departed ones, and giving promise of seeing them again, were sung. It was also obviously pleasurable for them, as they offered their praises, to consider the wonderment of living in a world without toil and heartache.

Sewell's gestures were emphatic and his voice carried the gospel out over the heads of the congregation as he became more engrossed in his message and particularly so when he led in song. He balanced the Bible in his left hand and pointed and waved and gestured with his right, and he stared fixedly with squinted eyes at some in the congregation. His look was a little fearful, and sometimes AJ thought he was addressing him personally.

He was the best dressed among those present and the only one wearing a store-bought suit although it was now showing signs of wear. AJ remembered his watch chain, that dangled from his vest pocket and flipped up and down as he waved and pointed. He remembered him leading in song and, at peak, his off-tune voice carried to the roof's underside spilling out the windows into the countryside. The fact that he couldn't carry a tune was now accepted, dismissed, and no longer brought a smile. Overall, AJ remembered his obvious sincerity and how worked up and animated he became as he instructed his flock.

But the small congregation, comprised probably of about thirty adults, and representing most of the community, and now increased by two from outside the community, chatted quietly and waited for the sermon to begin. A few others remained outside and AJ guessed they had not been saved enough to come inside. They likely only came that far because of a forceful wife, and the congregation always prayed for them, in particular, at every service. Maybe one day they would come inside, and then the tears would flow when those sinners vowed to give up drinking and card playing.

What wonder is memory, for here, once again, but this time in AJ's mind, they all gathered and for a few moments, he was with them again.

There were the men dressed in loose-fitting bibbed overalls, with a white or blue work shirt underneath with collar buttoned, and most were wearing older-looking shoes. From some bib pockets dangled a string that was attached to a bag of roll-your-own tobacco while that of others bulged from a homemade twist. Many of the men were not clean-shaven, shaving being a tedious task, and most hands were muscular and gnarled from field labor. He remembered the worn-down, tobacco-stained teeth and the deep wrinkles causing their sweaty faces to look older than their true years, and how, being in church, they seemed to look cleaner.

Their wives wore ankle-length dresses; much like Sarah's, and a few wore aprons over their full dress. A bonnet covered some heads such as seen today on the heads of Amish and Mennonite women. Most all were plainly and similarly dressed and their salt-and-pepper hair was also pulled back and wound into the accepted bun that protruded through a hole in the back of their bonnet. Like those of the men, their faces and hands also revealed signs of leading a hard life.

And another point, an oddity, AJ remembered that most women held fans provided by the town funeral home. Waving them back and forth, sometimes in unison, the fans created a little breeze and gave a little relief from the hot, summery room. AJ positioned himself to catch the slight breeze created by Sarah's fan when the open windows gave no fresh air. Sometimes those windows had to be kept closed to avoid the summer insects, and AJ, distracted, or in a fit of yawning, watched and studied moths fly into the room and become drawn to the lamps. Their enlarged shadows performed a death dance on the walls before they got too close to the hot glass chimney and fell to the floor, presumably to their own hell, he reasoned.

Although in the minority, there were various aged children sprinkled among the group, and all seemed to behave. Each boy wore bibbed overalls, some outgrown, and the girls had on dresses likely homemade from print material.

Here, AJ would recognize his old classmates, who, like him, were now reaching adulthood. His eye would usually seek out Melissa, who was the prettiest person he had ever seen, but shyness and lack of courage never permitted an approach. "Lissie", as everyone knew her, would one day become an important part of his life, as would Lindsey and Kathryn Stone.

These people had only a little, and a paper dollar looked lonely lying among the coins in the collection plate. Still, they seemed richer in spirit than any others he would encounter in later years. It seemed God was with them all in that humble setting and His angels, although probably pulled off-key in song, may have accompanied the music.

Many years later he would think how wonderful it would be if he could return there for just a little while, to watch them and listen to their plain-spoken prayers. He envisioned them all now reassembled somewhere in that "sweet by and by" and in the land where they'd "never grow old."

This he knew, absolutely, that those making up that congregation were materially poor, but it didn't seem to matter on that day.

-§-

Chapter Six
Trouble

Contractors established camps for the foremen in the bottomland work sites, either large tents or sometimes a still standing barn; here he would meet his laborers to give daily instructions and distribute their pay at week's end.

Since the method of payment was often cash, usually distributed Saturday afternoon, a small gathering would commence after noon at such locations. With ready cash some of the workers would hang around sharing a bottle of moonshine, compliments of a thoughtful fellow worker who had secreted the contraband away during the week. A poker game was often started, and as the evening wore on, those remaining sometimes became boisterous, unruly, and easily riled.

Not uncommon, when alcohol overcame good sense, tempers would flare, creating a very dangerous situation. Sometimes petty arguments would escalate and fighting would break out. Word soon spread about these gatherings among the locals and it was rumored that one man had almost lost an ear when a knife-wielding opponent overcame him in one such brawl.

Sheriff Leonard Mitchell, Lenny to most, had proven to be a good law officer although he was limited in experience. Previous to the last election, when he defeated the seventy-year-old incumbent, Lenny had served as county road commissioner and spent an interim term as the justice of the peace, parlaying this later experience to his present position. Although sometimes a little overexuberant, he was alert to the potential danger from the holler gatherings, gave a good ear to every tale, and watched closely anytime outsiders came into town. His sometimes questioning of their intentions was more than offset by the friendliness of the shopkeepers, always appreciative for contributions to the local economy, but his overexuberance was often weighed against these benefits to the shop owners.

Word soon spread around the camp that the men were not welcomed by the townspeople, and some tension developed between the locals and the outsiders. The men spoke of Sheriff Mitchell as being particularly hard on strangers allowing this was due to his political leanings and questionable obligations, and they warned one another to be respectful if ever approached by him. Mostly though, both sides realized the presence of strangers was temporary and for the most part got along reasonably well, and strangers attending church now and then humanized the outsiders and eased the stress.

AJ had finished Saturday's chores and eaten supper and told Sarah he was going down in the holler to check on what work had been done the past week.

"Heard they've almost got the entire Polston land cleared," which they both knew was only a few miles from the old Garrett place, "and I'd like to see how soon they'll be getting to ours," he remarked in leaving the room.

"Aaron Joseph, now you listen to me, you watch your step and be careful, it's Saturday, and you know what they've been saying about those men, you got no business being 'round them, and you hurry back," Sarah pled as she rose from the table.

"I'll be okay, Ma, I'm taking Ring with me, see if he scares up some squirrels on the way," and stepping off the porch he headed for the road leading down.

Big Al was a newcomer to the work site, and only a few knew much about him. Then too, Big Al didn't volunteer very much about his background and always sidestepped specific questions about his past. They knew he was from "up north," never said anything about a family, that he had moved often, and supported himself hiring out at various itinerant labor camps. What they didn't know, and what shallow questioning had somehow failed to unearth, was that Big Al had served time in an Alabama penitentiary for rape and robbery, and was currently wanted for questioning about a robbery in southern Illinois, where he had, in fact, robbed and severely beaten to death a storekeeper.

He was mean-spirited and was avoided by others particularly after he had been drinking, when his foul mouth would spew forth with cursing, and he would become surly and defensive. More than once he had challenged others in argument, over something relatively insignificant, and displaying his favorite show of force, he would pick up a stick, scribe a line in the soil, and dare others to cross it. None crossed it out of fear and respect for his strong body and unpredictable mental state, and when Big Al infrequently ventured to town, even Sheriff Mitchell wisely opted to avoid an encounter for fear of setting him off. In so doing the local lawman may have lost the only opportunity in his career to capture a fugitive and thereby cementing his name as a past legendary sheriff.

When AJ came within sight of the tent he saw no one but could hear voices in the distance and there seemed to be a heated argument in progress. Old Ring, his dog, commenced a low, even growl, and AJ noticed the dog's neck hair bristle in a way he'd seen happen when the dog cornered a possum in a persimmon tree.

"Don't go near the men," his mother had cautioned and AJ took heed. He stopped and crouched behind some waist-high bushes, and waited and watched out of curiosity. His instinct was to turn and leave, but he felt safe from this vantage point, and was intrigued and curious about what was going on between the men.

He recognized one of the voices as the one they called Big Al, and the other, whose name he didn't know, sounded like the voice of one he'd previously heard at the worksite. The later was a wiry little Cajun man, thought to be from eastern Louisiana.

AJ had never heard such talk as was spewing back and forth between the two, and it was becoming more heated.

"You got the money, you ugly sonofabitch, and I want my half," the Cajun yelled.

"Go to hell, half-breed, shut up, and back off while you kin. I mean it now, I'll beat the hell out of you if I have to come after yeh, you no-good little runt," Al threatened.

"You don't scare me like the others, you fat pig, one way 'nother I'll get my money, yeh kin bet on it," and with that the Cajun came into AJ's view. He was backing away from Al, who was now edging closer and closer to the small man.

AJ froze and became nervous in witnessing the affair, not sure what to do. Never had he seen two adults so mad, and for the moment, he was dumbfounded as he watched Al swinging a massive fist that delivered a hard blow to the Cajun's head and knocked the diminutive man to the ground. Wiping blood from his mouth, the small man rose with startling quickness, and his hand went into his pocket, pulling out a shiny object, and with a click, exposed the thin steel of a long blade. Lunging at Al, whose eyes widened while he backed off, the keen steel found its first target across Al's cheek and drew blood. Al's hand went to his cheek and he looked at the palm of his hand with a look of disbelief and now, with fire in his eyes, he charged the little man with obvious intent to kill.

The Cajun, with a second swipe with the ugly weapon, drove the blade into Al's chest and more blood gushed from that wound. A look of terror came across Al's face and he turned away, took a few steps, and fell to the ground, holding his hand to his cheek and staring at the blood saturating his sweaty shirt. Although in great distress, he uttered no sound—the blade had deeply penetrated his heart.

Quickly, the Cajun grabbed a brown satchel off the ground and ran past AJ, and seeing him in passing, gestured menacingly with the bloody knife. Staring at him through steely, squinted eyes, and pointing the weapon, he warned, "Tell what you saw, boy, and I'll be back and run this here knife through you," and continuing when Ring bared his teeth, "you hold that dog or I'll kill it." With that, he quickly moved to the tree line and disappeared into the uncut timber.

AJ knew the other men were not far away, and hurrying past the big body of Al, now on the ground, face down, he ran until he heard the sound of sawing and spotted a group of men around the bend attempting to finish a section before quitting for the day. Among the group, he spotted the familiar face of Lindsey Stone, the man in church who had bought his mother's pie.

"Better come," he said with quivering voice. "Some men were arguing and fighting back at your camp, and I think one's hurt real bad."

"Who were they?" Lindsey asked, as they both headed in the direction of the tent.

"It was the one they call Al, and I don't know the other one, but he was a lot smaller than Al, and he cut Al with his knife. They were arguing over money, Al's hurt bad I think," AJ replied between deep gasps for breath.

Other workers managed to get Al up to the pike and load him into one of the service trucks, but on the way to the hospital, he died. Big Al left no means for the contacting of relatives and somewhere someone would always wonder what happened to him.

Lindsey patted the back of AJ's hand, in a gesture of comfort, and they both walked up the logging road and down the pike to the house to explain all that had happened to Sarah. AJ liked this man, and had not felt such closeness to another adult, other than Sarah, since his father died. It was the start of a long friendship.

Back at the camp it was discovered that there was no money available to meet the Saturday payroll as the little Cajun had absconded with over six hundred dollars. Despite Sheriff Mitchell's best efforts, using hound dogs in the woods, asking countless questions, and notifying counterparts throughout the state, the Cajun was never caught and became somewhat of a local legend in infamy, as one having murdered and gotten away with it.

A few days later, thanks to a county fund set up to deal with paupers, Al's remains were laid to rest, without marker, back in the corner of the cemetery. Brother Sewell said a few words, and led a few others in singing *Nearer My God to Thee,* and then they all prayed fervently for Big Al's soul as his pine-boxed body was lowered into the grave.

Chapter Seven
A Second Beginning

Lindsey would now often stop on his way to pick up a tool for the jobsite and if he saw AJ or Sarah outside the house, say hello, and inquire about how they were getting along. Although always seemingly in a hurry, he found time to stop for a few minutes, asked if they needed anything from town, and AJ and Sarah would look forward to his visits.

"Hey there AJ, you doing okay, I'm just heading to town, you folks need anything?" he would inquire.

"No," AJ replied, "but much obliged, can't think of a thing, can't afford nothing no ways." He continued by asking, "You here this weekend?"

"Yep, be here this weekend and a whole lot more it looks like, reckon I'll be here for quite a while yet, but we're making good progress the last few weeks, ain't seen you down there lately," Lindsey remarked.

"Been working hard to get corn in whilst the weather holds, still got a field of beans to get in; 'sides, last time I come down, almost got myself killed, hope that crazy man don't come back, he might be looking for me sure," AJ replied.

"You don't have to worry much, AJ, too many people looking for that man 'round here. Why'd you ask about the weekend, something going on?" Lindsey asked.

"No, nothing special, we just thought you might like dinner with us after church. I know Momma would want you, she cooks good, but reckon you know that," AJ remarked, smiling.

"Sure would welcome something home cooked," Lindsey responded. "Eh, say, AJ, I've been thinking, do you mind, eh, me, being 'round your ma, she seems friendly towards me, wouldn't want to offend, and..." Lindsey stopped.

"Ma acts different when you're 'round, you'd be welcomed Sunday," AJ countered as he studied Lindsey's expression.

"Well, now I got something to look ahead to," he said, and an obviously appreciative and smiling Lindsey climbed behind the wheel of the old service truck, started the engine, and slowly drove away.

Early afternoon Sunday, hours before they expected Lindsey to arrive, Sarah wrung the head off a plump Plymouth Rock hen and let the torso fall into a large washtub, starting the preparation of a special Sunday meal. Being unaccustomed to having guests, particularly someone outside the community, she was obviously excited and went about work humming a medley of favorite hymns. The meal would consist of the chicken, floured and fried in sizzling lard, sliced potatoes, getting their turn in the lard, green beans, flavored with the grease from a piece of jowl bacon, cornbread, made crusty by being basted with the grease, and sugar pie. Lindsey remarked it'd been a long time since he'd had such a fine meal and AJ and Sarah watched him devour multiple helpings.

The three sat on the porch for more than an hour after the meal, talking about progress at the dam, how the crops were doing, speculated about whatever happened to the Cajun, and sundry other subjects in the current news.

Lindsey related how he had recently visited his daughter, Kathryn, how much he missed her, and how he longed to be with her all the time.

"Why don't you bring the girl down to stay with us for a little time, bet she'd love to see where her daddy works? We've plenty of room," Sarah suggested, noting a look of further interest on Lindsey's face.

"Don't know if she'd leave my folks," Lindsey said, "but if you think it'd be okay, maybe she'll come," his voice seeming to beg for confirmation of the offer.

"'Course, it'd be fine, we've got an extra bed, and plenty of food. Be nice to have a little lady, someone other than this ruffian." She gestured toward AJ and smiled a little when she saw his reaction.

"Maybe I'll ask her, it'd be nice to have her 'round even for a few days or so. And I can't tell you when I have eaten such a fine meal, and how obliged I am for being asked," Lindsey said as he glanced at his pocket watch and stepped down from the porch. "My lands, where'd the time go, I'd better be leaving, I have some planning to do for work tomorrow."

Sarah politely rose and walked toward the edge of the porch, when Ring, who had been sleeping underfoot, awoke and saw something out in the yard. Lunging past Sarah, the dog brushed against her, causing her to trip and begin falling from the porch. Quickly, Lindsey grabbed to steady her, and for a single moment, held Sarah in his arms. Years later, answering teasing, she would blush and adamantly deny falling on purpose.

Lindsey would return for future meals, and would often be seen sitting next to AJ and Sarah in church, and he brought his daughter down to visit on several occasions. A warm relationship grew between the four, and it was generally accepted, and frequently discussed by the church matrons, that Sarah and Lindsey would ultimately marry. "Be good for both of them," would be the summary opinion, and AJ was pleased with the strengthening relationship. He saw happiness in his mother's face when Lindsey's was present and this pleased him.

Kathryn, Lindsey's daughter, now lived with her grandparents in the city, and didn't remember much about the time she had spent on their farm before her mother died. She was excited to learn about farm ways and tagged along with Sarah, was fascinated in watching her milk the cow, and proud of the opportunity to gather the eggs. She greatly admired AJ, listened intently as he pointed out wildlife, and seemed to absorb every word as he described his years in the bottomland. They had something in common; they each had felt the pain of losing a parent. It was impossible to conceive that many years later, little Kathryn would become principal of the local high school.

Almost a year passed, the year was now 1940. Franklin Roosevelt remained President by defeating Wendell Wilkie by a large margin of votes, seventy-two to six in the local polls, but no one dared speculate publicly who the six were, but much was happening in the world that was being discussed in the courthouse bench forums. For the most part, however, life went on as usual on the local scene. To most, rumors of war still remained in the realm of Bible prophecy but to a few who were more cognizant of worldly affairs, there was trouble in Europe. Hitler, quite possibly the Antichrist, was on his march.

One of the highlights of that spring was an announcement appearing in the church bulletin reading:

TO ALL IN ATTENDANCE, The wedding of Widow Sarah A. Garrett to Lindsey H. Stone will be held here at the church on Saturday April 20 at eleven a.m. Best man will be Aaron Joseph Garrett, Sarah's son. Singing by the Thomas sisters and banjo playing by their father, Harrison. Bring food for a pitch-in. Brother Sewell will perform the service and formally introduce his new wife to those who have not yet met her. Let's all show our love to Sarah and Lindsey by coming.

So it happened that they were married, and after a brief honeymoon in Gatlinburg, they returned and started making plans. Lindsey would continue to work on the dam until its completion, would move in with Sarah and Aaron, and as soon as the current school term ended, Kathryn would join them. During this period of adjustment, Lindsey revealed his desire to one day increase the farm's size, looking forward to the time when he would be farming full time.

Sarah had no insights that Lindsey came into the marriage reasonably well off financially due to a rather large sum received from the sale of his previous farm, and that he had increased the size of this nest egg through disciplined savings. Although it would take over ten years, ultimately, due to these funds and their good management, their farm would expand to over four hundred acres, the majority of which was tillable. But in those ten years, the world would change dramatically, and so would their little sheltered community and their lives.

For the present, however, planting had to be done, and the reaping and the storing of the crops and countless other farm chores. Fortunately there were now more hands around to handle the work.

-§-

Chapter Eight
Better Times

Billy "Tooch" Mullins and AJ were good friends, their birthdays were only months apart and they had grown up together. While AJ attended school, the two would pair up during recess, and when one was seen, the other was usually not far away. Also, Andrew Garrett and Sam Mullins, fathers of the two, grew up together and those two earned a reputation for wild behavior as young people. Two generations of the families remained close as they shared similar lives and later, after Andrew's death, there were many times when AJ faced a job requiring the strength of two, and it was Billy who usually showed up.

Now nearing eighteen, both boys, as would be expected, developed interests beyond farming and were often seen shyly eyeing the young ladies at church gatherings and on the town square. There they gathered with other young people, particularly on Saturday evening, and they formed a team of sorts. AJ was handsome but very shy while Billy, although somewhat homely in appearance, was very outgoing. It was he who would start the conversations with the young ladies, and AJ would later ease in, or be summoned in by an admiring girl. Later the two, lounging on the front porch and comparing notes, would discuss the relative beauty of the girls, and express what they would do if they only had the courage. But for now, the short conversations with the girls, and their beckoning smiles, remained exaggerated in the boy's postmortems.

Sometimes though the two would sit and reminisce about the numerous escapades they had shared when they were younger.

"Remember that time we were hunting squirrels and decided to make a swing out of that grapevine?" Billy asked as he started laughing.

"Coulda killed you," AJ replied, joining in the laughter.

"I don't think anyone knew what happened," and Billy went on, "they'd have taken the switch to both of us, remember how they warned us not to fool with the vines? I figured it had to be fun if they thought it was that bad."

"Well, we ended up knowing why, didn't we?" AJ added.

"I couldn't wait to cut the bottom loose, and remember how we argued over who'd get the first swing out over the side... Almost got in a fight, you finally got mad and said go ahead, and that you were going home, well, I sure got my way. I took that big run and was way out over the side, when the doggone thing broke loose at the top, that vine started coming down all around me, thought I was a bird for a minute till I hit the ground. Knocked me senseless, first thing I saw was you up there laughing, hell, I coulda killed myself." Billy now ceased laughing.

"At first I was going to leave you lying there, but then I felt sorry for you," AJ reflected.

"Remember when we threw the blacksnake in the Skaggses' outhouse?" AJ offered, and they both commenced to laugh heartily again.

"They never seen us hiding 'hind the hen house, if they had, they'd killed us, Mary Skaggs went in and let out that scream, came running out on high and pulling up her bloomers," Billy recalled.

"I always wondered if she peed in the outhouse or running back to the house," AJ said, as both roared with laughter, then paused and thoughtfully added, "You know, she coulda had a heart attack."

"Oh me, ha ha, how'd you think up doing those things, they never did find out it was you who let that bag of frogs loose in school during recess, either," AJ said. "And another thing, were you with me that time I doubled back to the schoolhouse during recess to get a drink and there was Bill Mitchell and Geneva Thompson getting ready to go at it... Wonder whatever happened to Geneva after they moved out. She sure was a good looker, wasn't she?"

"Sure was, I don't know, heard they moved north somewheres, her daddy found work up there, I think maybe in Indianny," Billy answered, and continued, "Another kid I wonder about was that little Leroy Strode kid, remember when we dared him to ride that calf? He was too dumb to be scared of anything. I think after the family quit hiring out to the Polstons, the whole bunch headed for Detroit, never heard nothing about them again, probably never will."

"If ole Leroy came back he'd probably be looking for us. I remember telling him he'd be just like Tom Mix iffen he could get on Polston's calf, and stay on long enough; he'd break it for riding. Little idiot didn't stay on that calf ten seconds when it dumped his ass off into that cow pile. Leroy said his daddy whipped him 'cause he could have broken the calf's back, not because of the smell," AJ related. "I guess he got off easy for the manure on his pants."

"We had fun back then, didn't we, AJ?" Billy contemplated.

"Yeah, but it sorta makes a person sad thinking about some things, don't it?" AJ said, and added, "I'm kinda sorry I did some of those things, and if Leroy was here I'd tell him I'm sorry, you know, he was sorta slow."

The boys continued their porch talk while watching the sky darken and the emergence of the bright stars and a full moon. The country insects began their serenade and the pond bullfrogs bellowed forth with their forlorn calls.

Finally AJ broke the momentary silence and said, "Billy, just thinking, do you believe God is up there in those stars or is He all around us all the time?" He paused before going on. "He probably wouldn't approve of some of the things we've done."

"Be ashamed iffen He was around *me* all the time, I think He's just up there waiting for us to come home, least I hope," Billy replied. He reflected on this thought for a moment, then added, "But He just had to laugh at Mary Skaggs waddling back to the house."

"You think we'll make it to heaven?" AJ then inquired.

"Yeah, I think so, 'specially me, not sure about you, but if I get there first, I'll speak good about you," Billy replied.

A yawn or two and the two broke up for the night, and Billy headed down the moonlit pike toward home.

A few days later AJ was in the upper pasture hauling rocks over to the side of the field to make plowing easier when he saw the gangling figure of Billy approaching from the pike.

"Here, AJ, you missed this one," he said in approaching, pointing to one among the many rocks still littering the field.

"Missed more than one," AJ replied, "don't know where they all come from, I pick 'em up every year and then there's ten times as many next year. This field's real bad, grows rocks better'n corn. Wish I could sell 'em, I'd be rich."

"Say, you like to dance? FFA's gonna put on a dance in the meeting hall Saturday. I just heard about it in town. They's inviting people from Summersville and Jimtown and I don't know where all else. Expect a big crowd. They's got musician people in from Nashville. Someone said they'd played in the Grand Ole Opry. Maybe you'd go with me," Billy offered.

"Dance, only dancing I ever did was trying to miss stepping on cow piles in the barn, don't think I'll be going to any dance," AJ replied.

"Well, just thought you'd like to know," Billy said, and with a sheepish smile, "by the way, I ran into Martha

Hendrickson in town, she was the one who told me about the dance, said Melissa and her was going. Said Melissa was sort of stuck on you, AJ, what do you think about that? Second thought, that Melissa's a pretty thing, doubt she'd be giving you a look."

"Eh, she said what, did she say anything else, like did Melissa say anything else 'bout me, I've never talked to Melissa much, just see her in church now and then, can't imagine she'd give me any attention, don't know if I'd be able to handle that." AJ tried his best to not sound too interested.

"So let's go to the dance, everybody's going to be there, you don't have to dance. Just watch ole Bo Jangles Billy and learn," Billy begged.

"Maybe so, Melissa, golly me, hmmm…" AJ's reply trailed off as Billy left, taking big strides across the field sidestepping the stones.

A Grand Ole Opry billing just about said it all among the locals. For years everyone in the area had listened to the music being broadcast from that country music shrine on their battery-powered radios. Only *Lum and Abner* and *Amos and Andy* enjoyed the popularity accorded music from Nashville, and to see someone live from there attracted people like magnets attracting metal.

The very young and the very old were there and many in between, and they gathered in groups as though assigned according to age. There was foot stomping and hand clapping to the music, and people laughing, and some ventured to the center of the room and performed dance steps spanning a century. Billy had paired up with Martha Hendrickson, abandoning AJ to a far corner of the room, where he sat and watched. He viewed Melissa from a distance but could not muster the courage to approach her.

Soon, Sarah and Lindsey saw him alone over at the side, and Sarah, knowing the shyness of her son, beckoned him over.

"Aaron Joseph, did you know your ma could dance? First time I've danced since before your pa and me married. Wish you'd dance with me," and with that she tugged at his reluctant body, bringing it upright. "Here, now do this," she added while calling attention to her feet, "do what I do, ONE, TWO, THREE, FOUR," and she repeated the cadence as AJ's clumsy feet and stiff body followed.

They managed to negotiate to the other side of the room and Sarah then pulled AJ over to Melissa, who was seated and trying her best to look indifferent to what was going on.

"Melissa, dance with this boy, I'm tired," Sarah said, and she left the two facing each other.

"Maybe we could just sit a spell," AJ mumbled with bowed head, and vowing not to make a fool of himself.

"That'd be fine. I'm kinda tired too," Melissa replied with a warm smile.

They sat and talked about everything except how much they admired each other, and although the subjects were sometimes silly, the ice had been broken. Although no dancing was done, the evening at the dance would be remembered forever.

-§-

Chapter Nine
War, Part One

The year 1940 was a good year for most, and particularly so for the Garrett and Stone families. Sarah and Lindsey wed; the farm increased in size due to an opportune purchase made by Lindsey of the remaining Polston tracts not covered by the water, and AJ and Melissa started seeing one another. Crops were planted and yields were extraordinary. But eclipsing everything else, and drawing significant attention to their change in lifestyle, was Lindsey's surprise purchase of a remarkable machine, a Fordson 9N tractor to replace Sadie and Sallie, and none too soon, as Sadie had almost lost her eyesight and Sallie had come to balk at work. The ageing mules had done more than their share, earned their keep, and had attained near family status. The barn would never be the same without the sounds of the ageing pair who had been the daily companions of Andrew.

Truly, God had blessed them all, indeed!

Soon the tranquility would end, but not quite yet. Now, it came to be that the courthouse bench forums seemed to always end up with discussions about whether or not Roosevelt was going to lead the US into the European war. No need, was the consensus of opinion.

"We don't have no business throwing in with those French and English and them other people, let 'em stay in their place and leave us be, we already fought one war for them," and most would nod in agreement.

The winter came and the following spring but they were seasons of unrest. Now it was spoken that things were breaking out in "Chiney," but a hunker-down attitude still prevailed among the locals. "Them people are all crazy, let 'em fight among themselves, let's stay out of it."

And summer came with the planting, and life continued to be good for most. There was church, there were weddings, Billy Mullins married Martha Hendrickson, and AJ stood up for his friend. The relationship between AJ and Melissa strengthened; now hardly a day passed when they did not see one another, causing people to whisper, "They might as well be married." Lindsey's little girl, Kathryn, adjusted to her new environment, and was doing exceedingly well in school. Sure, there was some apprehension in the air, but 1941 held promise of being still another banner year. Sadly, the apprehension of some was well founded.

Brother Sewell finished his sermon and parishioners were starting to fidget, in anticipation of their exit, when

Basil Strode charged in from outside. He had just come from town.

"Everybody, I just heard awful news," he shouted, "the Japanese have just bombed our Pearl Harbor. Hunnerts kilt. Nobody 'spected it; Roosevelt said we're a going to war against them and Hitler."

"Well, now they've done it," someone said, "them cowards, they'll be sorry, bet this thing won't last three weeks," and most seemed to agree.

At the onset, the changes were slow to come and there seemed to be general confusion as to what would happen next, but then changes *did* start and then they kept accelerating. Some remembered the first World War and the many stories that had been passed down from fathers to sons, stories of bravery and heartache and injury and death, and how a local boy, Sergeant Alvin York, had taken them all on, single handed, and came back a national hero. How he had won a Medal of Honor and had been given a farm when he returned, and this story encouraged support for Roosevelt's fireside announcement. "Boys, we need you!" the recruiter summoned and they responded; all the young men of the area were asking where they should go to sign up and boasting the enemy was in for a "whooping." But parents, in private conversation, spoke of Banner Qualls, the doctor's brother, who returned from World War I minus one leg and acted "kinda quare" the rest of his days.

AJ signed the paper as did Billy and countless other young men from the area, and they all raised their right hand, swore to abide by the rules, and then they waited fourteen days for the arrival of a bus that was scheduled to meet them in the courthouse square. It was understood it would take them to a train station in Nashville and from there they would be taken to an army camp and trained to fight a heathen enemy.

"Aaron Joseph, I don't want you to go over there," Sarah pleaded.

"I don't want to go either, Momma," AJ choked up and, clearing his throat, replied, "but I have to. You don't want me to be like that Moodyville man in the other war that shot off his foot so he didn't have to go, would you? Everybody's helping out. Anyways, word is you either go, or they come and get you and I couldn't abide by that shame. Hear say they need every hand, the country's in awful trouble. I'll be careful, and Lindsey will be good to you. Farm's in good shape, and maybe this thing won't last long, no matter, but I'll sure miss you and Melissa, and don't say nothing to her but I think we'll get married when I'm back, that is if she's willing, all this talk got her to crying last night, she's so softhearted. Something troubles me a lot, though, Momma, I don't think I can kill another human being, I hope it's right with God."

They hugged, and Sarah kissed her son's forehead.

On the day of departing some of the boys were cutting up; others were kissing and hugging loved ones, and shaking the hands of people they had been around all their lives. Preacher Sewell was there with them and they watched the arrival of the chartered bus pulling into the square, and its brakes gave a whoosh sigh of relief as it came to a stop. The bus was khaki in color, and painted in big letters on its side was *UNITED STATES ARMY*.

Sewell's voice rose above the noise of those who were laughing and others who had tears in their eyes.

"Everybody, let's take a minute in prayer," and the crowd became instantly silent as they waited for his parting oration prayer.

"Father, we're here today with loved ones and some will be leaving us, and we pray that You'll watch over them while they're away from us, and bring them back safely. And Father, we pray that You'll send Your Holy Spirit down to these boys and us, and calm the terrible fears and sadness in all our hearts. Stay with these good boys just like You did when You sent Your beloved David out to fight the giant Goliath, and guide them in battle like you did with Your servant Joshua, and help our boys to make the walls of those foreign towns crumble. We humbly ask these things in the name of Thy Son Jesus Christ. Amen."

And the crowd in unison softly repeated, "Amen."

As their names were called, the young men filed onto the bus, AJ and Billy seated side by side, and final good-byes were waved from the windows, and young girls blew kisses to their boyfriends. Soon the bus lumbered down the pike and young faces stared out the window, taking in final glances at familiar places, and recalling humorous and sad events that had occurred there. They tried their best to hide their sadness from others by lowering their heads, but they were young boys, and most had never been away from home, and tears filled the eyes of more than a few. Meanwhile, back on the courthouse square, the smiles had left the faces of those remaining. Instead, they quietly dispersed and returned home with heavy hearts.

Within the week a letter arrived, the first ever received addressed to Missus Sarah Stone.

Hello Momma,

Hope you and Lindsey are fine. The weather here is warmer than home. Just wanted you to know where I am. The train from Nashville took us to a place called Fort Bragg in North Carolina. Place is full of people all hurrying doing this and that. Everything was a mess in Nashville; we had to hurry from one place to another to get put on the right train. We got our uniforms and they have told us what building we will sleep in. There are rows and rows of these buildings all look the same. Beds lined up from one end to the other. They all have toilets indoors, ha. I am here now and tired. Things better get in order or we may not win when we get over there. Be here six to eight weeks. Got to go, we're going to mess, ha ha, that's what they call breakfast, dinner and supper. Let you know when you can write me.

I Love you, Aaron Joseph

Tell Melissa when you get my address to write me and I'll write her.

Being thrown in with the other young men at Fort Bragg was a cultural confrontation of cataclysmic proportions for AJ. Different dialects; some so pronounced he had trouble understanding their words, unfamiliar skin colors, red, black, and yellow, social and cultural backgrounds all totally foreign to him. He thought about the trouble the biblical people had building the Tower of Babel and figured it must have been something like this. Could such a diverse group ever work together, he wondered.

But boot camp was quickly underway, with all its structure and commands, and soon all the differences were not important. They became color blind, color of skin no longer made a difference, a Bronx dialect got no more attention than that of the boy from Alabama, and the Jewish boy's prayer was accepted alongside that of the Catholic. AJ could see that there was no allowance for individualism in the army.

Hello Momma,

How are you, hope doing fine. I'm okay. Well, I been here almost three weeks now and they are keeping us busy. Learned how to take apart a gun today, then we went to the shooting range and practiced. I did better than a lot. Most of the people here are from big cities up north, and I don't think they have done much hunting. Can't shoot straight. Some try to make fun of me in a nice way but I don't pay them much attention. Got to tell you this, one boy from New York City asked me about milking a cow 'cause he'd never seen it done. Told him you just turned the knob and milk would come out, ha. I think he believed me. We marched for two hours yesterday, sure got tired but not tired as some. Had one boy faint. I've got a lot to tell you but not much time. Tell Melissa I'll be writing her, and tell Kathryn to write me and tell Lindsey I said hello. How is the lake coming? Also, give my regards to Brother Sewell. Also I ran into Billy two days ago, he said they were going to transfer him to something called special services. He may have to go somewheres else.

I love you, Aaron Joseph

And the following night AJ penned another letter as yearnings welled up within him as he missed the closeness of home. Never before in his entire life had he been away from his mother a single night, nor from the friendly sights that he knew so well. These people were so different from him and he struggled to understand the way they talked and acted.

Dear Lissie,

Well, I am writing from Fort Bragg, North Carolina, where the weather is fine. How are you? I hope you are well. I have been here more than three weeks now and in six to eight weeks our training will be over and we will have a weekend off. I sure do miss being with you, Lissie, and I hope you miss me. Lots of people will be here to visit when our training is over and I sure wish you could come and see me then. I reckon I will have to go someplace in Europe when I'm done here but I may not be able to say where even if I know. They are not letting us write certain things, they say we could tip off the enemy, ha. Please write me and tell me you can come as I am counting on it. In this letter is $30. That should be more than enough for your bus ticket with maybe some left over for whatever you need. I sure miss everyone. Tell your folks hello.

Love you truly,
Aaron XXX

A watch could be set by his arrival from out of the darkness. The drill sergeant's voice broke the quietness with his deep, roaring voice. "Reveille! Reveille! Rise and shine, soldiers, up and at 'em, skinheads, time to get up. Yeh'all got five minutes to hit the grinder or you'll do push-ups. Now get at it, you, now, what the hell you doing in that sack, haul your worthless ass out to the grinder," and so it went every morning.

And the former bunch of casual, straggling strangers now fell into line as one, in rows of two abreast, and they marched off to mess. It was five thirty in the morning, the welcome sun would not rise for another two hours, and the cold air filled their lungs. The day would be another one for marching and crawling under barbed wire, and stabbing dummies hanging from a pipe with a gun's bayonet. Fortunately it was unseasonably warm for this early February day and this would ease the physical stress.

HUP, two, three, four, HUP two, three, four, now follow your left, your left, your left, right, left. Their minds repeated the cadence and their feet carried them to mess, that consisted this morning of fried potatoes, chipped beef, and gravy, mingled and piled on the metal partitioned plate. Actually, AJ took a liking to this hearty fare, and others marveled at the gusto with which he ate, whispering and smiling to one another that he was half starved when he joined the army.

The sergeant was one of the meanest-spirited humans AJ had ever encountered, but was more civil to him personally than to others. He recognized that AJ did what he was told, carried out orders smartly, and caught on quickly to military ways.

The melding together of the various cultures, ethnic values and customs did not come easily to this odd assembly of young men and friction sometimes arose, particularly after a hard day of exercises.

They had marched most of the day, the exercise requiring that they ascend a forested incline, reach a point some twenty miles forward, pitch tent and remain outside for the night, this all to allegedly simulate battle conditions. The young men were dog-tired and irritable as some sat around a circle in one of the larger tents passing the time by playing poker for pennies they had scrounged up among themselves. AJ's inexperience with the game showed, and he was mostly contributing to the wealth of others—that is, until fate placed four kings in his hand that he proudly displayed, laying claim to the large pile of pennies.

"Hey, ridge runner, where in hell were you hiding those cards?" came a challenge from a voice from among the small circle of players. The inquiry had come from a streetwise young man of foreign descent from the Chicago area, and his tone was serious.

"You de one what dealt 'em to him," chimed in Lemuel Farmer, a burly young black from Alabama, smiling in response.

"Didn't ask you, nigger," came back the Chicago lad.

"We don't like that word, mister," Farmer responded, and adding, "Tennessee here ain't good enough to cheat."

"Don't care if you like it or not, just don't forget your place, and don't talk if you ain't asked. Understand that?"

"Don't want no trouble, you just calm down, don't make a fool of yourself, white boy," Farmer answered, as he started to walk away from the small group.

Feeling put down and embarrassed, the Chicago player rose and hurled a final insult, "Don't walk away, boy, or I may have to make you clean my boots from now on."

The Chicago lad's movement toward Lemuel was a terrible mistake because one painfully hard blow was thrown to Chicago's face, causing his knees to buckle, and he dropped to the ground, trying to shake the blow off. He wisely spoke no more, realizing that he was greatly outmatched by the manual labor-steeled body of Farmer, who was now being restrained by fellow soldiers. Justice had been served in its lowest form and such encounters were sometimes ultimately necessary to melt the differences between the races and cultures among the recruits. In time, however, they would all become as brothers and this incident would be forgotten until it was painfully recalled on a distant battlefield.

Through crude physical stress the recruits became bodily fit soldiers, and come to have the rudimentary skills necessary to fight equally the enemy on the battlefield. Truckloads of new equipment, in seemingly never-ending lines, rolled into camp daily, and still more buses came packed with wide-eyed young men from the farms and the big cities, and they alighted from the buses, fell into irregular lines to answer roll call, and shuffled into the newly erected barracks built to accommodate them. This scene was being repeated all over the country as the nation rolled up its sleeves and geared for war.

Throughout all this AJ, like the legion of others to follow him, became physically hardened but his gentle spirit secretly asked if he could kill another man.

Just as the base was growing, so were the small towns nearby as they geared up to receive the scores of soldiers who visited when they received passes for a few hours off in the evenings. New taverns sprung up, and following this concentration of young men, there came an element heretofore unknown to these Bible-belt towns.

Recruit Tom, an adventuresome boy from New Jersey, had come to like AJ. It was almost an example of opposites attracting one another. He admired AJ's honesty and laughed at AJ's expressions when he would relate farm incidents that were totally foreign to his big city upbringing. He also had not known anyone reaching their respective ages so lacking in knowledge about things so commonplace on the city streets. AJ liked Tom as well because he saw in Tom a person with deeper feelings than projected, and qualities of goodness and loyalty in him. They paired up for their first weekend off, hopped on a bus, and it soon let them off at the small nearby town's Greyhound bus station.

"Let's get us a couple beers to start things off," Tom suggested, then continued, "Guys back at the base said there's a little place down from the station, has beer for twenty-five cents a bottle."

"Never tasted beer," AJ said, continuing somewhat boastfully, "We drink moonshine down home." AJ's drink was limited to a swallow he had received one Saturday evening back home on the courthouse square. The liquid burned his mouth and throat so badly that he decided he didn't care much for drinking alcohol.

"We'll just have a couple," Tom explained, attempting to imply that his usual intake was several more, but in this instance saying one or two would do. And then he went on, "Maybe we could take in a movie, or how would you like to get some, I hear they got several cathouses in this town, guys back at the base say the gals are clean."

"They got what?" AJ asked.

"Cathouses, man, whores, prostitutes, you know about them, don't you, Tennessee?" Tom questioned him with disbelief.

"Oh, them, no, I'd rather go to the movie if it's okay with you. You know you can get a disease in them places, 'sides, I don't hold to that sort of thing. But maybe a beer would be fine and the show sign said they're playing a Randolph Scott western tonight," AJ replied, while avoiding eye contact with Tom.

"I like Randolph Scott, but let's get that beer first," Tom pleaded.

They had their beer, and AJ pretended to enjoy it, saw their movie, and returned to the base.

Mail call was special and a sinking heart always followed when a name was not called, signifying the absence of a letter. Some never received mail and AJ noticed their attempt to hide their sadness and embarrassment, and you never asked them why no one wrote to them out of respect for their feelings.

"GARRETT, AARON JOSEPH," the call came and AJ anxiously started to take the perfumed envelope from the clerk, who teasingly withdrew it from his grasp for a moment, smelled it, smiled and handed him the letter, whereupon AJ sniffed it, and then retreated to a private corner to open it.

Dear AJ,

I'm so happy to get your letter. I've been missing you a lot. Not been much to do here since all the boyfriends are gone. I sure hope this thing don't last long. In town yesterday there was talk about the war not going well. Don't you get hurt.

I can't wait to come there and see you. Let me know more details about where to go and when and I will be there. I love you so much. I received the money but am returning it as I had saved up enough from helping do the tax records at the courthouse. I ran into your momma and Lindsey in town yesterday and they told me they had gotten mail from you. That Kathryn is sure a pretty little thing. I guess the dam work is going along okay. Lindsey sure takes care of Sarah, don't he? Seems like he can't do enough for her. Martha came over for a while last evening. She said she had gotten word from Billy that he was being transferred to do something special. Your momma told me that you had told her about him getting transferred. Lord, I hope he is not being put in something more dangerous. Martha cried and I didn't know what to say. I don't know if I should be telling you this but she is going to have a baby. And I don't think Billy even knows so if you happen to have any contact better not say anything just yet. Well, I have to go help Daddy out in the barn so I will close for now and look to get a reply from you soon. Don't get hurt. I love you. XXX
Melissa

It was both a happy occasion and a sad one. Melissa arrived Thursday evening on the Greyhound bus and AJ was able to meet her as his formal training had ended that day, and the soldiers had the evening off. The wide-eyed little eighteen-year-old girl, who had never been this far from home before, had managed the trip without difficulty, and she now descended the steps of the large vehicle into AJ's welcoming arms. She was a naturally beautiful girl, whose face had never known makeup, and her brown hair was tied back by a blue ribbon. Under a thin cloth coat, she wore a new floral print dress she had purchased just for this trip and it was drawn close to her waist by a fabric belt of the same material. In one hand she held a brown purse borrowed from her mother, and in the other, a flimsy piece of corrugated luggage. AJ hardly noticed her dress but instead stared at her face and bright smile. They embraced and kissed as would be expected of two young people falling more deeply in love, and AJ thought that he would die if necessary to defend her.

After checking Melissa into a small hotel, recommended by a chaplain on the base, they proceeded to a little sandwich shop, sat and talked for almost two hours, and in the background a jukebox played a song about a strawberry blonde and a medley of tunes by the Andrews Sisters.

Tomorrow the soldiers would assemble at the base at oh nine hundred for roll call, fall into parade ranks in their dress uniforms, and smartly march to the tune of "The Caissons Go Rolling Along." Standing on a flag-draped parade stand was the base commander, looking splendid in his dress uniform, that sported a chest full of medals and ribbons, and a state senator and his wife and daughter.

Saturday they ate breakfast together, took in an afternoon movie and attended a dance sponsored by the local townspeople for the graduating soldiers. They held hands and reminisced about the only other dance they had attended back home. They talked of their families and common memories and what they intended to do when AJ returned. It was there, in the lobby of the small hotel that they decided that they would marry and they hugged and kissed as though it would be their last, and from there to the bus station, and they reluctantly parted.

The bus left at two in the afternoon on Sunday after they had spent the morning together. As the big gray vehicle pulled away, AJ saw Lissie's face peering out the window and noticed the tears streaming down her cheek. Good-bye kisses were thrown from the lips, and the bus pulled away heading north and west on its circuitous journey to take Lissie back home. Although there would be occasional letters, this would be the last time they would see one another for almost three years.

On Monday morning, after a routine reveille, they stuffed their duffel bags with their personal belongings, and after a trip to the mess hall, they lined up to board the buses that would take them to a train depot, and then a troop train would deliver them to a point of embarkation on their journey to overseas.

-§-

Chapter Ten
War, Part Two

Over fifteen hundred men from all parts of the nation and from training bases strategically placed to accommodate them, mustered in on the dock shaded by the shadows of the enormous troopship that would take them overseas. The men looked up in awe at the huge vessel, eyeing it from stem to stern while waiting their turn to board. AJ had never even seen a picture of such a ship, much less boarded one, and he marveled that such a weight of steel could float on water. It was simply difficult for him to accept.

"Hope we make it to where we're going, guess we'll be going through waters plum filled with German U-boats and sharks," one soldier remarked.

AJ overheard and asked, "U-boats?"

"German submarines," came the reply, "they call 'em U-boats, they wait around out there under the water, and shoot ships with their torpedoes, one hit, the ship's a goner, blows it to smithereens."

"Do you know anyone running into one of them U-boats?" AJ asked with widened eyes.

"Hell no, thank goodness, just read 'bout them, hey, they're calling our unit, we'd better go," and he walked ahead, leaving AJ fearful about ascending the gangplank.

Hours later the ship, loaded with its cargo and its complement of troops, slowly moved out of its berth, out into the harbor, and then out to open sea. The men stood at the rail watching the shoreline disappear with nervous eyes, and before nightfall, there was no longer land to see. AJ had never been out of the sight of land and felt uneasy by its disappearance, realizing how precious the earth was to him, and he longed for a handful of Tennessee dirt to sift through his fingers.

They had been at sea for four days and by now the floors had become decks, the walls of their sleeping quarters, bulkheads, and their beds, racks. The racks were stacked one on top of another with only a foot separating the lower from the upper and gave a suffocating feeling to some. Although no U-boats had been sighted, the great ship moved into a storm at sea and was tossed to and fro as though it were a small toy boat. The heaving of the vessel grew worse and men were getting sick, even the more experienced sailors on board, but to a greater extent the many soldiers who had no sea legs at all.

"You okay, Tennessee?" Tom Manning asked AJ. Their racks were side by side and they had retreated to their assigned sleeping quarters lying down to seek refuge from the creeping sickness epidemic affecting their comrades. One by one they watched other soldiers rise and run to the latrine, a trough that was flushed constantly by running seawater. If they happened to be on deck when the sickness came, the sailors warned them to run to the fantail and hang their heads over the rail before they regurgitated. "Either get there or *you* clean it up," they threatened.

The power of suggestion, from observing others racing by, and even the mere question of one's condition, was the fateful trigger that finally caused AJ to succumb to the dreaded feeling.

"My stomach's churning, I think I'm gonna puke," AJ responded, and with that, he, Tom following closely behind, quickly retreated to the toilet, where they found little relief in losing their last meal. AJ could not remember a time when he was so sick, and it stayed with him throughout the night and well into the next day, until the sea once again grew calm.

They had been at sea for eleven days, having left Brooklyn, New York, on February 19, and now, with one sailing day away from their destination, stomachs began to mend and many of the soldiers had gone topside after the noon mess to enjoy the calmness of the sea and the sunshine that bathed the deck. A light but unseasonably warm breeze made it pleasant to be outside and watch the immense sea that surrounded them. While it was mid February, the warmth in the air gave a false feeling that all would be well, but anxiety persisted about where the ship was headed and what peril lay up ahead. Generally, though, the banter was lighthearted as the men shared stories about their past experiences and the places they were from.

Suddenly the loud clanging of a bell alarm sounded and the tempo of activity instantly changed as the sailors rushed hurriedly to man their assigned battle stations, and the soldiers scurried aside to get out of their way. Over the loudspeaker someone screamed, "PERISCOPE SIGHTED, OFF STARBOARD BOW," and the ship began to turn sharply to the port.

Everyone's eyes strained as they looked off in the distance but nothing was sighted except the white caps of small waves. Some guessed it had been a mistaken sighting but later it was learned that indeed a periscope had been seen by a sailor standing his watch, and that the ship had commenced evasive maneuvers. This news caused great tension to remain for the next few hours, as all on board stood ready to react to whatever would follow. Finally, the fear subsided when it became apparent that no danger was imminent.

For whatever reason, they would never know, possibly a U-boat out of torpedoes, or on orders to just spy on them, but the submarine had opted to pass this opportunity to check off a kill. Still, the event served to forewarn that somewhere out there an unknown enemy had designs to kill them.

In time the men would learn that the British ship *The Duchess of Atholl*, which had been their safe haven for twelve days, had not been so fortunate the following October when a German torpedo found its mark and sank the stately liner.

But later that day the soldiers lounged in their racks, some were on deck hoping to witness the first sighting of land, and still others sat at the galley tables dashing off letters to loved ones that would not be mailed for weeks.

They were all waiting because word had been passed down that the captain would soon be making an important announcement concerning what would happen to them when the ship reached its destination.

Not long after, a sharp whistle over the loudspeaker and the firm voice of the captain was heard. "Your attention please, this is the captain speaking. I hope you men have enjoyed your stay on *The Duchess of Atholl*, my crew and I have been pleased to have you aboard these past days, but our long journey is soon to end. Tomorrow, March 2, for those of you keeping track, at approximately thirteen hundred, we will arrive at our destination, that is, I am now authorized to say, Belfast in Northern Ireland. After our ship is properly docked you men of the 34th Infantry division will disembark, by unit, and on shore you will board waiting buses and be taken to a base in Northern Ireland. Your unit commanders will be in possession of your orders. Good-bye and may God be with you."

As they had boarded the ship, now they disembarked, looking like a column of ants following one another down the long gangplank, some glancing back for a final look, and they proceeded to the line of waiting buses. They would head north to a training facility still being constructed, where they would join young men from England, Scotland, and Ireland, and collectively all would prepare to add additional support to the invasion of North Africa, that currently was still on a small scale.

After several days, late one evening, a tired and homesick AJ had an opportunity to write his first letters from this distant land.

Hello Momma,

Well, I wanted you to know that I arrived safely and I am now in Northern Ireland. I hope you and Lindsey and Kathryn are well. We have been in constant training so I am very tired. We came over on a big boat that they said was a vacation liner. It was about ten times longer than our barn. Coming over, I got seasick and was laid up for two days, but I am okay now. Almost everyone got sick, even the sailors who were used to rough water. The people here are very friendly. The ones I have met remind me of people back home. We got to go to a little town last evening and they all were asking me where I come from. They never heard of Tennessee. I got to talking with two men who are potato farmers here. They wanted to know what we grow and a lot of other things about the soil and weather.

I should be here another two weeks and then we will go to somewhere in North Africa. It looks like I may be in the thick of things but I feel I will be okay. I guess what we're about to do is very important. There are boys with us from all over these parts. Some wear dresses with nothing on underneath, ha, but they warn nobody better make fun. I will explain later.

Did I once hear Dad say that the Garrett people were from Ireland? I saw our name on the front of a store when we went into a little town the other night. Who knows, they might be kin. I sure miss everybody back home and wish I was there. I know God is with us, but a prayer from back home will always help. There is so much to tell but I reckon when this is over I will have the time to fill you in. You can write me at the return address on the outside but the letter might not reach me for a while, so don't

worry if I don't answer quick. I love you, Momma. By the way, how is the water coming?
   Aaron Joseph

And to the other person he longed to be with:

Dear Lissie,
   I had a little time and wanted you to know how much I miss you. I am here in Ireland and will be for a few weeks. Everything is fine and I hope you are well. I just wrote Momma so both of you should receive a letter about the same time. I hope you are waiting for me to get back. I sure do miss everybody. The people here are nice to us and all but it is not like being home. We went in to a small town the other night and a man paid for my dinner. I will be anxious to get a letter from you. My address is on the outside but I may not get a reply for a while, as we will be leaving here to go to North Africa. I heard Billy is already there. A boy was with him in training but got transferred back to us and he said he heard that is where they were headed. Someplace called Casablanca. He may already be facing the enemy. I don't understand it but somehow the French are fighting us there. They are a different group that has sided with the Germans I think. I don't know how that could be. We have heard we are against the Italians and Germans. I hope he has been able to write Martha. When you see her tell her I will be looking for him but I hear it is a big place. I am interested in what is going on there so write soon. Tell everyone hello for me and if anyone wants to they can write me. Would you look in on Momma and all and make sure they are not worried about me? Well, I better go as they are saying we

*should turn out the light now so I will say goodnight and
I love you. XXX Write soon.*
Aaron

While the training was similar to what the men had
grown accustomed to, the intensity was now increased
and they were daily told to train hard, that their lives
might depend on the skills they were acquiring. Today
they would be crawling under barbed wire with
rumored live bullets possibly whizzing over their heads,
and AJ crawled forward as close to the soil as possible,
hoping he would not get shot and that the soldier with
the gun would keep it trained to the high side.

As this particular training session progressed, in a
nearby field, there was arriving a khaki-colored staff car
at the base gate, and after a brief stop, those inside the car
returned a quick salute and the guard nodded for them to
proceed, whereupon it drove forward and finally
stopped at the base headquarters. A high-ranking officer,
carrying a brief case, hurriedly got out and entered the
building and those watching sensed that this visitor was
possibly bringing news that would affect them.

Later that day the hungry but tired men marched back
into camp, where they washed themselves and waited
for their turn to go to evening mess. AJ, who had just
finished washing, was sitting on the edge of his bunk,
when the training officer stepped into the barracks and
loudly summoned, "GARRETT, AARON JOSEPH," and
then, "FARMER, LEMUEL, you men, report to the base
headquarters."

AJ and Lemuel, the young black, who had challenged
the Chicago bully back in basic training, both reported to

the waiting officer, and the three proceeded to the headquarters building. AJ looked at Lemuel, asking why and looking for the reason they had been called out, but received no response other than a shrug from his comrade.

The mystery visitor from the car now sat behind a metal desk in the center of the room, with its walls covered with maps, and warmly greeted them as they entered.

"Gentlemen, I'll get right to the point. You two have been selected from among your unit as possible candidates for a special operations activity in the planning stages. We consider your selection an honor and it's based on the proficiency you have maintained in your training to date. We're looking for only the best soldiers among us, and only those who have a strong desire to be a part of this elite corps. We propose to assemble our country's first Ranger Battalion, comprised of five hundred high-quality and willing soldiers, are you each interested?"

AJ studied the man and tried to determine his sincerity while all the time thinking of the repeated caution he had heard from others about the dangers of volunteering. Finally, concluding this to be an honest man, he asked, "Sir, what does a Ranger do?"

"Son, Rangers will train and become an elite squad of fighting men, like the British Commandos; in fact, they'll be trained in Scotland by the Commandos, if you haven't heard of 'em, I'm telling you, they're the best damn soldiers on our side today. They're tough sonofabitches and get difficult jobs done and soften the battlefield for comrades to follow, but this type of service isn't for everyone, it's tough!"

Although AJ didn't understand some of the jargon, he replied, "I reckon that'd be fine for me, sir, that is, if you think I'd be good enough, I don't think of myself as much of a fighter but I'd be willing to give it my best."

The officer turned and looked at Lemuel for an answer.

"Well, just wondering if I be okay with the others, I mean, being black and all," Lemuel asked.

"Farmer," the officer sternly responded, "we don't see the goddamn color of a man's skin in the army, we see good and bad soldiers, we must think you're good, and goddamnit, you'll do just fine."

Lemuel Farmer became the first black Ranger recruit.

Chapter Eleven
Meanwhile, Back Home

Rationing of many goods had started back home. Little books with stamps started to circulate, a coupon for this and a coupon for that. The courthouse square forum had a lot of fun talking about rationing when they learned each would be allowed only a pair of shoes every so often. They reasoned, "Hell, we couldn't afford to buy shoes noways," or, "Who wears shoes down here?"

Finally, listening to the remarks of the others, one quip got the heartiest laugh of all when, with squinted eyes, one looked up from his whittling and seriously asked, "Just what are shoes?"

The gasoline rationing didn't matter much either, as few owned automobiles, and enough gas was available for the farm equipment, that was about all they needed.

Excepting for the absence of the young men, and those draft-exempt individuals who left to head north to work in the defense plants, little change was noticed in the day-to-day activity of the folks remaining. Weekends and holidays would see the plant workers streaming down home for a few days with the family, and infusing some of the city wealth into the rural economy. But they were also bringing back subtle concepts that would affect life after the war.

But in the cities, the changes were much more evident. Factories originally designed to manufacture cars and sewing machines were now turning out tanks and guns, and these plants, formerly provinces of the men, now had female workers as well.

Young city men had also gone to war, and to acknowledge their absence, their families proudly displayed a card in their windows with a star, symbolizing each child that was in the service.

Cereal boxes offered rewards of model warplanes to the children and cowboy and Indian games were replaced by games emulating war and at school, children licked the backs of war stamps, pasted them in a book, and looked forward to the day that the filled book could be exchanged for a war bond.

The country had ramped up for war and revealed its awesome economic strength, and after the war would ascend to a powerful new position in the world hierarchy.

Meanwhile, back in Tennessee, Lindsey spent much of his time laying plans for the spring planting. He oiled and greased virtually every moving part on the Fordson tractor, dickered for the best price he would pay for seed, and attended meetings to learn of the virtues of proper crop rotation and soil conservation.

The water was now rising in the hollow and low spots had already disappeared from sight forever. Water was now covering where the Garrett house and barn had stood and soon these structures would become only a memory. Lindsey's job, working to prepare the land for the water, was almost over, and his primary interest was now in developing one of the area's most prosperous farms.

Overlooking its destructive nature, and the emotional trauma it brought, it was easy to imagine that the water would someday create an idealistic setting as it was seen lapping the sides of the steep hillsides and exposing the sheer cliffs of stone. Furthermore, there was the prospect that the coal oil lamps and the washing boards could one day be put aside, giving way to the electric bulb and washing machines, and those other things that power would bring. Lives might be a lot easier when all the poles, following the routes of the gravel roads, were strung together and the power became available.

Melissa came by the Garrets' often and she and Sarah would sit and talk and share information they had received from AJ, both longing for the day he would be back with them.

"Did he tell you they were sending him for some special training in Scotland?" Melissa asked.

"Yes, he told me, I'm so afraid for him," Sarah replied. "do you suppose he'll be in more danger?"

"I don't know, they said in town he was probably going to be like one of those policemen in Texas," and after a thoughtful pause, "I don't know why they would need police over there," Melissa offered.

"Well, maybe some of the boys act up and have to be straightened out, you know how they can be, I dunno, doesn't sound too bad a dealing with our own," Sarah speculated. "Honey, how old is your brother Harold?"

"Why he's seventeen going on thirty," Melissa replied, smiling, and then thoughtfully added, "Be out of school next June, why do you ask?"

"I reckon he won't have to go, do you think?" Sarah offered.

"Surely not, this thing'll be over by then, Lord, I don't even want to think about that. I wouldn't mention that to Momma and Daddy."

"You're staying for dinner, won't you?" Sarah asked.

"If you'll have me, I'd be much obliged," Melissa replied to her future mother-in-law, of whom she was becoming very fond.

Almost every day, but always on Saturday, men would stop in at the hardware store and discuss news of the war's progress. And if you happened to miss the round table discussion, there was always the evening news broadcast over the battery radio with reports delivered by Lowell Thomas and Gabriel Heater. They learned that there was something called radar that someone had invented. It was able to see faraway airplanes even at night or in the fog. "Guess it's better than what they had at Pearl Harbor," someone speculated.

They were outraged and vehemently opposed to the news that the government was going to start taking taxes out of a man's pay before he got the money. The forum would never accept the necessity of such a thing, but were calmed by the reasoning it was a temporary measure to fund the war. "We voted them in and we can vote them out," was the consensus.

"I hear our boys are getting ready to attack North Africa, and did you hear, that Mullins boy may already be there," one remarked and adding, "fitin' there's hot and heavy, I hear tell,"

"Sarah Garrett said her boy was heading that way and then they sent him to become a police, don't seem to be the right place for Aaron Joseph Garrett, always seemed too gentle," came the reply.

Had they only known the truth, they would have found it inconceivable that their local boy, whom they had seen around town and at the mill getting corn ground into meal, or out plowing in the fields, was being trained to become a killing machine.

Meanwhile, in front of the house, and close to the pike, the buds of a near-fifteen-foot maple tree, the one Sarah had named Aaron Joseph while in a pensive mood, were swelling and making ready to serve as a harbinger of the oncoming spring season.

-§-

Chapter Twelve
War, Part Three

The staff car took AJ and Lemuel to the train station, where they boarded one of the passenger cars of an ancient steam-driven train. It headed north and east to a port on the Irish Sea and there a ship took them to a coast city in Scotland, then the arduous journey would continue and finally end up at their destination in Achnacarry, Scotland. They were two of the six hundred who remained of the original fifteen hundred volunteers and after their bodies had been physically challenged to the extremes, more so than in their entire lives, only five hundred would survive who had mastered the rigorous challenge. Both AJ and Lemuel had done so and they, and their comrades, would comprise the elite group of soldiers known as the 1st Ranger Battalion.

Since they would be an amphibious landing group, the men were transported to the western shores of Scotland, where they learned the skills of landings from the sea to fight against the enemy in all types of weather and during the daytime and at night.

It was August 1942, and the men assembled for roll call, and after becoming accounted for, they were addressed by an unfamiliar officer. He needed fifty men, he said, to join Canadian and British forces, and together they would perform a significant offensive in Europe. They would be the first American ground soldiers to see action in Europe as they executed the raid on the French city of Dieppe. Neither AJ nor Lemuel was selected to be a part of this group but they, as well as many others, learned a great deal later from the postmortem discussions about the failed raid.

"You know, the sonafabitches pounded our ass at Dieppe, wherever 'n hell that is," one remarked.

"Yeah, I know, some of the guys didn't come back, didn't have a chance. What the hell were they trying to do anyway, hope to Christ the big guys plan the next one better, or leave me the hell out of it. Stupid sonafabitches. The krauts knew we were coming, hope the hell we learned something," came the ranting reply.

"Know any of the guys that didn't make it?" the first asked.

"One guy was from Iowa, musta made his family happy as hell for their son to be one of the first killed," the second remarked.

"Things might get better with Eisenhower heading it up, and Darby's always been watching out for us," the first offered.

"Maybe," the second replied.

Rigorous training would resume for over the next two months, the men were getting tired of the drills, and the grousing would continue, but both men and the planners continued to hone their skills for action the following month. They would perform a landing assault at the Port of Arzew in Algiers, North Africa. But at this time, this information was not known, although the announcement would soon come.

The men stood at ease, knowing that Darby would soon be speaking, and as expected, he arrived and vaulted himself onto a temporary raised platform. He told them that he knew that they had trained hard but the training was necessary for the operation to follow. While not specific, he alluded to the fact that it was to be an amphibious night landing on an important seaport and that the operation would be called Operation Torch. The men were not told that the port was the Port of Arzew in Algiers. Darby explained that Churchill had originated the idea quite awhile back as a way of diverting the Germans from the European fighting, that President Roosevelt agreed with the plan, and now they were going to do it.

The job of the Rangers would be to land and take out two German gun batteries, allowing troops to follow with less resistance and ultimately capture nearby Oran. He said he was proud of their effort and was confident in their ability to get the job done but unfortunately, due to the sensitivity of the operation, they would not be allowed to send any mail to those back home until the operation was complete. As AJ contemplated what he had heard, his emotions were mixed between being prideful of being able to be a part of something so important and being fearful of facing imminent death. He hoped his fears were not evident to others.

Now they broke ranks and over the next few days busied themselves making ready for their first confrontation with the enemy and the stark realty that they could be killed.

Darby would report that the trip toward North Africa was not unpleasant except a short span of rough seas had sickened some of the men. AJ avoided this second bout with the dreaded upset stomach but he watched the familiar parade to the rear of the ship by others. The men exercised and target-practiced by shooting at objects thrown into the sea, and they speculated about the events to come. Briefings were held and they now learned all the details of the proposed assault, the planning seemed thorough, and they were pleased to finally know the details of the task ahead.

On the night of the landing, the men sat quietly as they waited their turn to board the small landing crafts, formerly anchored to the ship's deck but now bobbing in the water beside the ship. A heavy fog made it difficult to see much beyond the little boats, and they heard distant noises and wondered if the same thing was happening on ships nearby. AJ took his turn climbing down the rope ladder, just as he had done in training exercises months before, and took a seat in the little boat, leaning on his rifle, that he held tightly between his legs. His friend, Farmer, had maneuvered to get into the same boat, apparently feeling more secure near someone he knew.

"Reckon I look like you now, Farmer," AJ said, hoping to ease Lemuel's tension and hide his own. He was alluding to the soot-like substance that he had used to cover his face and the backs of his hands.

"You definitely better looking," Farmer replied with a broad grin.

"You think we'll be all right?" AJ asked.

"Be fine, ridge runner, ole Lemuel gonna take good care of you, gonna keep us from getting shot. Gonna be just fine, we gonna make history," Farmer reassured.

Soon they heard the scraping of the boat's bottom on the sandy beach and in the darkness waded into the water to get to shore. They remembered from the briefings that one gun battery would be to their left and the other to their right but that the upper one was some distance up a rise. Neither battery could be seen because of the fog and darkness that still enveloped them, nor had they apparently been seen. They had met no resistance to this time, and the men were surprised and relieved given the pre-battle information they had received. They wondered about the French soldiers feeling secure and half asleep in their gun emplacements.

Suddenly, however, gunfire, a sniper from somewhere in the darkness had spotted them. Then more shots and shortly they heard bullets impacting the side of their boat with a metallic *ping, ping, ping,* and they knew they were under fire.

Wasting no time, the sergeant quickly gave orders, "You, you and you," he pointed with a broad sweep at about twenty of them, "you guys, head to the lower gun battery and silence it," then he went on, "and you, and the rest of you, up that rise over there, I want that upper battery eliminated." AJ would head up the hill wondering what he would do when he reached the top. Could this be his last climb up a hill? Strange, that under these conditions, he would think of the many times he had scampered up the hills at home hunting squirrels with the dog, and odd, upon observing a vine hanging from a tree, he would remember swinging on a similar one.

Zing, a bullet cut through the night air so close to his head that he heard it pass by, and he shuddered at the closeness. This was it, he thought, and he strained his eyes to see if he could tell where the shooter was. Another flash from a firing, this time revealing it was from someone in a tree about halfway up the hill. The sniper had tried his best to kill him and failed, and suddenly, there was no hesitation about what he had to do.

Like a squirrel sitting up there, a gray squirrel, only this time the squirrel was shooting at *him.* He carefully aimed his rifle and with no second thought, pulled the trigger. The unknown foe dropped from the tree and was heard to hit the ground. AJ did what he had to do to save his own life and the lives of others; the act was fearfully simple, and so horribly depersonalized.

"You got the sonfabitch, I think," a nearby soldier said, adding, "Let's get the rest."

"God forgive me," AJ whispered.

They would reach the top meeting minimal resistance, and finding the entrance to the battery, he and several others confronted a group of French soldiers who were totally surprised that the enemy had gotten this close. Their hands were raised and they peacefully surrendered.

In all, over sixty prisoners were taken by this assault. The two gun batteries would no longer pose a threat to the scores of invaders that would follow, and the mission of the 1st Ranger Battalion was deemed a total success. Other troops to follow, attacking from several directions, would likewise meet with great success and their effort would be publicly acclaimed by President Roosevelt, Eisenhower, and the national press, and at a time when hope and reassurance were greatly needed. The success established a strong Allied presence in North Africa, causing the French to side with the Allies for the remainder of the war and the success served to significantly demoralize German troops to be faced later in battle.

They were sitting on the beach talking and attempting to rest, letting their adrenaline slowly subside; each soldier relating an account of some bit he had played in the heat of battle, when a boy from another company joined them. The newcomer had heard AJ referred to as "Tennessee" and it caught his attention in passing. Seemed his unit had reached this point by approaching the gun emplacement from the opposite side of the hill and he related that he had come all the way from Pennsylvania, "to wipe out the damn guns," and that his unit had been in North Africa several months. They had been fighting other French troops in a place called Casablanca and he reported they had suffered many injuries and some casualties.

"A guy in my company was from Tennessee," he said, addressing AJ, "from some little town in the eastern part I think."

AJ quickly looked up and asked, "Do you know his name?"

"Matthews or Milligan, I think, never got to know him well, liked to hear him talk, full of stories, poor guy caught some shell shrapnel, hurt pretty bad. Last time I saw him he was lying unconscious on a gurney waiting to be put on a ship, might not have made it," the soldier recounted.

"S'pose his name might have been Mullins?" AJ asked.

"Yeah, that's it, Mullins, do you know him?" the soldier inquired.

"I think I might," AJ replied. He bowed his head in deep thought about Martha and Melissa, and his momma. The odds were incalculable.

The sun was just now starting to rise in the east, and AJ glanced at his watch, noting that it was oh four hundred, their attack had started at oh one hundred, and he calculated it had taken them three hours to do what they had done. Then Lemuel approached bearing his trademark broad grin. "Told you we'd be okay, didn't I, ridge runner? Everything's gonna be just fine," he said, and AJ welcomed his presence and the sound of his voice. This had not been a good night for him.

For Billy Mullins the war, as far as AJ knew, had apparently ended, but for AJ, it had just started as time would see him in a behind-the-lines night raid on Tunisia and other raids designed to pave the way for General Patton's troops leading to ultimate victory in North Africa.

Following North Africa, he would be sent to Italy, where he narrowly avoided death on the Anzio beachhead, a fate many of his friends and comrades failed to avoid. Here he witnessed the anguish and suffering of others, it was here that he summoned the help of medics when Lemuel Farmer fell, and he could only pause for a moment and watch his friend expire in the arms of a distraught comrade. Was it him, he wondered, was it really the Chicago boy at Lemuel's side…crying?

The Chicago boy's face was drawn and tears were streaming down his dirty face, "Farmer took my bullet," he said. "He pushed me down and before he could get cover he was shot, I can't stand this damn war anymore," and when AJ went on past, Chicago was still sobbing uncontrollably and acting to comfort the dead man.

AJ would remember the horrors of Anzio forever, as the time of Lemuel's death, the time some of his friends were taken prisoner never to be heard of again, and the time he would be reassigned to the 2nd Ranger Battalion and participate in the invasion of Normandy.

It was early June 1944, and AJ had been promoted to the rank of sergeant and transferred from Italy back to England to help train new Ranger recruits. Knowing that he had recently tasted combat, and had actually evaded real enemy fire, the new men listened intently and respected what he had to tell them, and his slow, deliberate approach to training lent credibility to his delivery.

And while they trained, they looked about and it became obvious to them, watching the mountains of supplies being amassed nearby, that something was up, but most speculated that an invasion of the mainland of Europe was about to take place in the Balkans.

"Sergeant, what the hell's the army going to do with five tons of toothpaste?" a recruit asked as he laughed about a nearby mound.

"Well, Ranger, haven't you heard, we're gonna brush every tooth in the German army, don't want 'em to have rotten teeth, want 'em to smile when they surrender," AJ replied, and they both laughed.

"Another thing, have you heard this, I hear Patton's now here in England. Got appointed to head up the 1st Army Group, but there's no such thing. Somebody said they're building shacks and parking junked tanks and jeeps all around, said it looks like a damn base all by itself. Bet Patton loves to parade his ass around ghost town, ha, ha, ha."

"I understand it's to give the Germans something to talk about, they'll spend so much time trying to figure it out, they won't have time to think about us, that's about how I figure it, now let's get back at it," AJ ordered, but being amused at the thought of the pistol-packing general walking about a vacant encampment.

Finally it became known. AJ was requested to attend an important meeting on the morning of June 3. He remembered the date because he had received several letters on that day from Sarah and Melissa, most dated mid May, having been backlogged somewhere along the way.

"Y'all probably been wondering what's going on with all the buildup," the colonel started, and continuing, "Well we're heading to Germany, and on June 5 we're gonna hit France with one of the goddamndest invasion force any army has turned loose on an enemy. Now here's the job of the Rangers. Garrett, now listen up. We'll be among the first to go in, right here," he said, emphatically pointing to a large wall-mounted map of a beach at Normandy, and reemphasizing, "this section right here," jabbing with his pointer at a smaller section that had been labeled *Omaha*.

"This is where we're going, about a mile from Omaha Beach, on LCT's, and here's our mission. See this point here, we'll be trying to get as close to it as we can. Here's why this place is important, it's called Pointe du Hoe, wipe that shit eat'n grin off your face, soldier," the officer went on, somewhat agitated, "I said Hoe, H O E, now Pointe du Hoe is a hundred-fifty-foot high point overlooking the beach, and sit'n on top of Pointe du Hoe are three 155mm guns capable of strafing the entire beach, could give big trouble when the other boys come in, and they'll be right behind, so we don't have a lot of time. We've got this hundred-fifty-foot cliff to climb," a blown-up photograph of the area was shown, "then we got three guns to destroy before they raise hell with our men, then we got to hold the position till the rest of the army gets there. Are there any questions?"

"Sir, about how wide is that cliff?" one Ranger asked.

"Probably about four hundred feet wide, it won't be crowded with your skinny asses, should be an easy climb, 'bout like the hill at the far end of the base we've practiced on," the officer answered with the hint of a smile.

"One other question," another recruit asked.

"Yes," the colonel snapped back.

"Sir, did you spell that H O E?" and laughter broke out among the men as the colonel threw up his arms and dismissed them from the meeting.

The channel water was choppy the 4th and fast-moving storms moved in and made the situation worse on the 5th. The men hunkered down and held on tightly while the little boats rolled in the high waves. Word was passed down that the assault, now labeled D-Day, might have to be called off unless the weather improved, and with this rumor, some of the men breathed a sigh of relief, others voiced disappointment, or attempted to convey that image, while others uttered expletives and expressed feelings that the operation should not have been started in the first place until the weather had improved.

But late that day they noticed a calming and occasionally sunshine broke through the thinning clouds. Now they heard that the assault was still on and they should commence to inventory and secure their gear for the offloading, which would be upcoming within two hours. Quietness came over the men as each commenced to ponder what was up ahead, and the adrenaline started to course through their bodies again as they checked off in their minds their instructions. Some could be heard quietly praying.

They were about fifty yards from shore when the first shell whistled past their little boat, followed by another, then another. Then all hell broke lose, explosions ahead of them, beside them, and one boat had been hit and its men were scattered into the water. Life preservers were thrown to some, and in panic they grabbed at them and any other floating objects, as they tried to stay afloat. AJ looked over the armor-plated side of his boat and saw red splotches of blood in the water and one man being pulled out to sea appearing helpless, and he quickly disappeared. He reasoned their gear was heavy anyway and when it became water soaked, only the strongest swimmers would be able to overcome the weight and make it to shore.

More shells, and then they finally reached the shore and the ramp was dropped that would allow his men to rush forward. Now the rifle fire grew heavier and, looking to the side, AJ could see little holes being formed in the wet sand where the bullets hit. *Pling, pling, zip,* the sounds seemed so harmless, but he knew that any one was capable of ripping through his body and could end his life. "Stay low," he yelled to his men, "and follow me, hurry, let's get out of here."

They all crouched and ran forward, barely avoiding a large shell finding its mark inside, and the missile was heard to rattle around the interior before it exited through the boat's bottom, leaving a gaping hole, and quickly the small craft filled with seawater. The men looked back, after the smoke cleared, and they saw that the unfortunate pilot had been blown into the sea by the concussion of the blast, and his war had ended. Indeed, they were in great danger.

Crouched low, more than a hundred men from several LCT's, and all vulnerable from shooters above, crept toward the cliff, and AJ's squad in the forefront finally reached the base. Immediately they commenced to seek ways to climb the steep incline and, fortunately for them, were able to move into a sheltered area where the cliff's crown jutted out over the lower part, preventing the German riflemen from establishing a line of fire. For at least a minute, they could consider the best route to the top.

"Over there, there's a ravine," AJ saw a rutted section that was full of jagged crevices created by erosion and there was a smattering of gnarled cedar trees that had managed to take root despite the harsh environment. "We can grab 'em and pull ourselves up," was his guidance to the others. They rushed forward.

Leading the way, he and four others commenced the climb, and after a short distance up, they looked back toward the beach and viewed the appalling sight of scores of troops falling onto the sand, succumbing to the hail of gunfire from above.

Now about halfway up, they came to a bare area without handholds and had to stop for a moment to consider their next move. AJ noticed that just above the bare area there was a very large rock, and if they could just reach the point where it rested, it appeared the rest of the way to the top would be an easier climb. The Germans, likely positioned at the top, were unaware of their presence this far up the side, because had they been discovered they would have become easy targets of the enemy riflemen.

"Throw me that rope," he asked the soldier down below. "I'm gonna throw it up and around that big rock sticking out, see if I can get ahold of it; if I can, we can pull ourselves past this bare area." The coil of rope was passed up from below, from one man then to the next, and finally to AJ, and he formed a loop at one end, and after two tries, managed to lasso the rock. He tugged on it hard, to confirm it was secure, and then rappeled himself to the next level. Now, from this vantage point, he could see the entire beach down below and see hundreds of ships anchored out to sea that were sending streams of LCT's to the shore. He could also hear the deafening reports of the big German guns that were firing their shells at the ships, and at the small boats that were filled with troops. He fully realized the importance of silencing them.

Three of his four men followed his lead and reached this point but the rope had become abraded by the sharp edge of the stone and broke from the weight of the fifth Ranger. It gave way and he tumbled to the bottom, where he was assisted by medics and those above watched and hoped that their friend was not killed.

They were about thirty feet from the top and only an overhang separated them from the waiting Germans. Surely, AJ thought, if they pulled themselves on up and over the top, they would be seen immediately, and would become easy prey, so after pondering this predicament, he pulled his walkie-talkie from its patch pocket and summoned the field commander, asking for help.

"I see you, stay put, we're going to try and put some rounds in the area above you. When you hear the shooting stop, haul ass over the top, and you're on your own," the commander instructed.

And shortly thereafter a hail of explosions sounded as shells fired from one of the ships rained down above them, and then it stopped. With that cessation, AJ and the three men quickly clawed up the remaining distance and were now able to see where the Germans had been. In an entrenchment there lay four bloodied bodies of young German soldiers, and halfway to one of the gun batteries, another lay sprawled on the ground. There were also bodies of several Rangers who had apparently succeeded in reaching the top by taking another route but had been felled by those Germans who themselves became victims of the ship's exploding shells and now their twisted bodies, some with missing body parts and others with insides exposed, posed no harm. The vision of this carnage would be burned into AJ's memory, but for now, there was no time to consider the horrors of war. *My God, help me!* AJ thought,

The German guns were continuing to fire in rapid succession but those responsible were inside the emplacements and apparently felt secure, not knowing that their exterior was unguarded. Their guards now either were destroyed, or had retreated back to their main lines.

AJ motioned to the others to come forward and decided that, in turn, they would run forward and throw grenades into the entrances of the three gun batteries, one after another. AJ went first, the grenade was accurately thrown, and he quickly retreated to his men. They waited and counted—five, four, three, two, one—and then, a deafening blast, the bunker shook and smoke and dust poured from the entrance, and the gun stopped firing. The Germans inside were dead and entombed.

Apparently hearing the blast, a German soldier emerged from the second bunker with a drawn revolver that he pointed at AJ standing not thirty feet away. AJ heard two clicks as the handgun searched its chamber for a bullet to fire, but there was none to fire and a surprised look of terror came on the German's face. He dropped the spent weapon, turned, and ran down the hill, probably waiting for a bullet to penetrate his back, but no one had the will to shoot this terrified man from behind.

"We shoulda shot the sonafabitch," one soldier remarked.

"Maybe he'll spare one of us later," someone replied.

Now, in turn, the second and third large guns met the same fate as the first, and it became eerily quiet, except from the distant small arms fire coming from somewhere over the hillside.

Other Rangers were crawling up from over the cliff's side, like ants coming up over the edge of a table seeking a grain of sugar, and there was fear in each man's face, making it obvious they were ready to fire at anything that moved. It was probably fortunate that no men were lost to friendly fire. And soon the remainder of the Regiment massed on the Pointe du Hoe; it was now theirs.

Assembled, these men found themselves alone with orders to hold the position until the shoreline was secured. For two days they hunkered down in their newly dug foxholes, high above most everyone else, with limited food and water, and drove back several failed counterattacks by the Germans trying to recapture this important position.

After Omaha Beach was secured, it was determined that the Rangers had lost ten of their finest young men. AJ would one day receive a commendation for his efforts at Pointe du Hoe.

Within days after that area was considered secure, the push was on to drive through France, and compared to what the men had been through, the taking of the remainder of France was almost pleasurable as war goes. Every little town greeted the soldiers as they drove through the narrow streets unmolested and they felt as welcome guests of honor. The laughing and kissing and hugging of the French citizenry would soon, however, become a fond memory, as Belgium loomed ahead.

Massive numbers of troops were gathering for what would become known as The Battle of the Bulge, that turned out to be the biggest battle of the war. AJ had never seen so many troops, much greater than those who massed for the Invasion of Normandy. Scuttlebutt had it that over five hundred thousand men were readying for battle against an even larger German army.

It was now December 1944 and AJ, with one hundred fifty others, was directed to carry out a scouting mission, requiring them to go to a place called Malmedy. Nearing there, they emerged from a forested area and observed a small farmhouse in the distance. As the group marched closer they could see, with field glasses, someone near the barn and could tell that it was the farm's apparent owner feeding his livestock. AJ looked forward to this potential encounter, anxious to exchange farm stories with the first farmer he had seen since the start of the war.

But when the farmer saw them, he commenced to gesture for them to go away and this seemed odd to them, for most of their encounters had been with welcoming, friendly people. No mistaking it, this one did not want them on his farm, and his gesturing grew more pronounced the closer they drew to him.

Now, some hundred yards away, they realized that the man was trying his best to warn them to turn back, and the reason became obvious because pouring out from behind the barn, the house, and from their flanks, were scores of German soldiers. AJ and his men had allowed themselves to become hopelessly surrounded, and they raised their hands to the sky and laid down their arms.

The Germans came forward, pushing the men aside, and collected their rifles, placing them in a central pile, poured gasoline upon them and lit them with a match. An inferno consumed the wooden portions of the arms, reducing them to a pile of twisted metal while AJ and his men looked on in dismay and wondered what was to follow.

The men were herded into a tight circle with German soldiers, arms at ready, surrounding them. Off to the side, they could see an SS officer talking to another, presumably trying to decide what to do with their POW's, and were not sure.

Shortly, after what appeared to be a heated exchange, one nodded to the other apparently signifying agreement, and the other stepped forward and loudly commanded the men to remove their backpacks, and other gear, and move to an open area in front of the wooded area from which they had come. Probably, the men thought, they were about to be searched for additional weapons so they did as directed with AJ standing in the perimeter of the group.

No sooner than they had reached a point some twenty yards from the woods when the horrible sound of firing submachine guns commenced, and individuals in the group of soldiers commenced to fall to the ground, some of their bodies almost severed by the blast of bullets.

A bullet had torn through AJ's right side and he likewise fell in the farmer's field, and as he lay there losing blood, and only half conscious, he thought this farmer's field might be a good place to die for he was reminded of home. A blurred image approached, it was Billy Mullins, he thought, or was it Brother Sewell, he wasn't sure, so he kept quiet and the figure stood over him a moment, then moved on past. A short ways further, the blurred figure pulled a revolver and shot a soldier on the ground he had observed moving. For some reason, he passed over AJ, and while the Germans now assembled near the farmhouse, perhaps getting ready to move out, AJ crawled unseen to a pile of leaves in the wooded area and watched through dazed eyes until he passed out.

AJ was not sure how long he had been unconscious but he commenced to regain his senses when the morning sun penetrated the limbs of the trees, and he looked toward the farmhouse and then studied the area where the men had been slaughtered. The bodies of the men were not there, but the earth had been turned, and it became obvious to him that his friends had been buried in a common grave. At least, the German troops were gone but there was no activity around the now tranquil farm setting, and he wondered if the farmer had also been killed. It was all like a bad dream.

He lay there for the greater part of the day, dazed and unable to move and for a while again lost consciousness. He had a dream that he was helping his father, Andrew, cut timber, and he was being shown how to use the saw, and his mother, Sarah, approached and told him to mind himself, and to come on back home, it was time for supper. When AJ emerged from the dream state, he found himself crying uncontrollably.

Now, looking toward the farm, he saw the farmer returning from somewhere, and the wife had spotted her husband and emerged from the house, arms waving, and hurriedly ran to meet him. Where had he been, AJ wondered, and could he somehow get their attention, and would they be friendly if he did? He remembered the original encounter with the man and being waved on but he was desperate, and managing to get hold of a long stick, he weakly waved it at the pair.

At first he remained unseen, but then he noticed that the pair both looked his way and were talking to one another. They began to run in his direction and then he once again passed out so had no knowledge of what happened after that.

But the next time he awoke, he was inside and was lying on a strange bed and he felt clean. He looked across the room and saw a great fire in the fireplace and felt its warmth. His limp hands lay at his side and he could feel the straw that had been used for the mattress ticking. *This is like home*, he was thinking, when the farmer's round-faced wife approached the bed, and she bent over him, and swabbed his forehead with a washcloth that felt nice and cool. She smiled and spoke.

"American, we thought you would die, we cleaned your wound, there is no bullet, it went through, I go to get Papa, and fix you some soup."

When her husband entered the room, AJ saw that the man was very big and strong, with hands that had apparently endured much manual labor. This time he was smiling and he patted AJ's hand with his big hand, reassuring him that he would recover, and now they needed to get nourishment into his body.

In broken English, he spoke, "You know, I tried to warn you not to approach the house," he said, and continued, "your men, I am so sorry, I cried for them," and he could say no more as his voice cracked and his eyes filled with tears.

In their care, AJ got better each day during the eight weeks he spent with the Gasperau family. It was now

March 1945 and they had learned from neighboring farmers that the Allied and Russian forces were closing in on Berlin and Hitler himself, and that the end of the war was imminent.

He got to know the couple well during his recovery period by sharing stories about their families and their farm lives. They wanted to know about his mother, and about the way they lived back home, and the things they grew, and more about the impending dam and the changes it would bring, and on and on, their interests were insatiable. They made him promise to keep them in his heart when he would leave and told him about their son. "We have Henri, about your age," they explained, "our son, he's been fighting with the French underground in Paris, and now it's almost over and we want him to return to us," they added.

It was a beautiful day when the jeep pulled up in front of the farmhouse and picked AJ up. After hugs and kisses from the Gasperaus, he got in the jeep and they drove to a nearby newly created base, where AJ spent hours relating his experiences of the past months and in the debriefing session, his every statement was carefully recorded. The documentation would become very important when the fifty or so Germans playing roles in the Malmedy Massacre were put on trial. AJ later learned that the participants had all received the death penalty from the trial, but he found little comfort in this information or from the Purple Heart Medal he received.

-§-

Chapter Thirteen
Going Home

He had seen all the war that he wanted to see, he was going home, and he felt very fortunate. The soreness had left his body, and he exercised with the other men on board the troopship that was carrying them home. While studying the mess hall menu, for the upcoming week's meals, he noticed that today's date was May 4, 1945. Had it really been that long, had he been away for three years, and had he not seen anyone from home in that time? He wondered about the changes, and how would it be back on the land where he had grown up? He knew the old home place no longer existed; Melissa and Sarah had kept him up to date through an irregular but continuous stream of letters. The water had risen to its planned depth, and had totally covered the old Garrett farm, and he would never see it again. What else would he never again see? He would never see and talk to Billy Mullins, a thought that overwhelmed him, Billy's body had been returned for burial three years ago, and Martha, with Billy's child, had remarried.

And there were events burned into his memory impossible to repress, such as the memory of having shot and killed a man who fell to his feet from a tree perch, he tried to forget witnessing the face of his friend Farmer as he lay on the ground dying, and he tried to forget the fear inside him as he scaled the cliff at Pointe du Hoe, and the sight of the pieces of German soldier bodies scattered on the ground, and more than anything else, he tried to forget standing within his group of buddies and watching as they dropped from the German gunshots at Malmedy.

Before their ship docked in Boston it was announced that Germany had formally surrendered to the Allies, thereby ending the war in Europe, and when they disembarked from the huge liner, the men were greeted by a military band and friends and families who had waited patiently for the arrival of their loved ones The men hurriedly came down the gangplank to find moms, wives, children and girlfriends running toward them seeking to embrace with tears of happiness in their eyes.

From the deck, AJ's eyes scanned the crowd, not expecting to see a familiar face, it had been over two weeks since he had heard from home, but then his eyes rested on a lonely figure standing to the rear of the mob below. A blue ribbon dangled from the wide-brimmed straw hat the girl had on, and she was wearing a yellow print dress with a white belt around the waist. Her shoulder-length hair was blowing in the gusts of wind and a broad smile came across her face when she realized that AJ had seen her. She was more beautiful than he remembered and he would never forget details about how the solitary figure looked on that dock that day. Now he hurried down the ramp, quickly picked his way through the crowd of happy people, and grabbed and kissed Melissa again and again, and she cried tears of happiness. While they were embracing, AJ looked over her shoulder and only then did he see Sarah and Lindsey standing in the background. From the arms of Melissa he shook Lindsey's hand and now embraced his mother, and this time *his* eyes filled with tears.

Arrangements were now finalized; they would return to the hotel, he would necessarily board a bus that would take him on a route lined with celebrating spectators to a nearby base. Sarah, Melissa, and Lindsey joined him there two days later for a special ceremony on the base. Unknown to AJ, Sarah had received an itinerary of the events from the base commander and she and Melissa had excitedly looked forward to the reunion for over two weeks. It took them four days to get to this huge city by train, and every day was an eye-opening experience that they would recall over and over for years to come.

During the ceremony at the base AJ was presented with the medals he had earned in combat, a medal of commendation for his effort at Pointe du Hoe from the army, another medal of some sort that the French had added, and a Purple Heart for his injury received at Malmedy. After the ceremony AJ handed the medals to Sarah, who studied them for a moment and passed them on to Melissa and then to Lindsey, and then they were returned to their little blue boxes. When AJ returned to the barracks, he placed the medals in the bottom of his duffel bag, and years would pass before they were reexamined.

His orders called for a fourteen-day furlough, after which he was to report back to Fort Bragg, where his army career had started, and what seemed like a hundred years ago. He was to spend the final year of his enlistment in training new recruits in Ranger skills, all the time hoping that these young men would avoid the trauma he had gone through. Meanwhile, in the Pacific theater, troops were massing, hinting that an attack on Japan was nearing, and the end of the war was imminent, and he felt sorry for those soldiers not yet home and still facing death.

They seemed the shortest fourteen days he had ever spent, days spent walking the farm with Lindsey, or stopping by for a visit with neighbors or quick trips into town where he would renew acquaintances with someone he hadn't seen for some time. Although little was known about his service record, he was received as a local hero with hugs, handshakes, pats on the back, and "glad to see you back" from countless longtime acquaintances.

The courthouse whittlers were still there, they wanted to know all about the war, and the people "over there," and did he have to fight in any battles, and would he have to go back, and what did the boys think of Harry Truman, and on and on, but, as was his nature, AJ replied with as few words as possible.

On one such visit, he ran into Martha, who was holding her young son, the child of his best friend, and he was taken aback by the resemblance. They had coffee in the restaurant on the square and talked of Billy, and when they parted, AJ was glad to have crossed this sad and dreaded encounter. The evenings were given over to Melissa alone, and they discussed their plans when he would finally return for good. Without question, they loved one another very much.

Things just don't seem to be the same, he thought; the people he knew and loved, they were the same, but just everything else, he couldn't sort out what, it was just a feeling he had and he was troubled and concerned but he didn't understand. He asked about certain people, only to find they had decided to remain north, where they had found work. Entire families were now gone, people whose names were chiseled on the church corner stones and their names entered in the tax records, and on headstones in the cemetery, gone and no longer a part of the community. Farms had changed hands, this was what had allowed Lindsey to expand their place, but it was sad that the old names were erased. Then, there were all the things the war had brought, the rationing, and the talk of the battles, and the killings, and they had just heard that a horrible new weapon had been successfully tested somewhere out west.

And the land itself was different and familiar places were gone, some parcels were now under many feet of water and would never be trod upon again. And along the pike the light poles lined up to carry the magic power to those able and willing to pay.

But despite these changes, and the uneasy feelings they caused, AJ regretted having to return to the army base, wishing instead to just melt back into the comfortable routines of the farm, and be among the people of his small town. He knew this was where he belonged; it was the only remaining place that made sense to him, and he didn't want to leave Melissa, nor his family and friends, ever again, but he had to return.

Back at the base three months later, he was becoming more at ease with his new routine, and he commenced a countdown when his enlistment would end. He only had about three months to go when he would return home for good, and helping the time pass more quickly were the weekend visits from Melissa.

During one such visit in late July they were sitting in a restaurant and most of the people were discussing the latest news of the war. One diner approached AJ, patted him on his shoulder and said, "Hey, buddy, dinner's on me, just want to thank you guys, got three small kids at home, maybe they'll have a better world."

"Much obliged, I hope so, but hey, it's good of you, but we don't want you to buy our meal," AJ replied, feeling embarrassed by the offer.

"Nonsense, I'm buying. Say, while I'm here, what you think about Truman's ultimatum to the Japs, you think they'll give up?" he asked.

"I really don't know, hope so, sure wouldn't want to have to invade Japan, those people are desperate," AJ added.

"Maybe they'll throw in the towel, is this your girlfriend?" he asked, smiling.

"Yep, soon as it's over, we're getting married, right, Lissie?" AJ said, and he looked at Melissa for confirmation. She blushed, smiled, and nodded yes.

Bedlam broke out when they heard the news. It was late evening on Sunday and a great commotion developed throughout the camp. Half-dressed men came streaming out of their barracks celebrating and generally became almost riotous as they smiled, shook hands, and slapped each other on the back. They concluded the war would soon end because it had been announced that the air force had dropped a new super bomb on one of Japan's major cities, the bomb that had been rumored as unbelievably powerful, and it had brought about almost total annihilation.

"How could they drop it at night, not seeing the target?" one asked.

"They didn't, it's morning over there, damn, the thing blew the whole city up, my God, all those civilians," someone responded.

"Yeah, those civilians who've been making weapons to kill us," another joined in.

"Maybe I'm thinking about all the kids, Lord, war is really hell," was the thoughtful response.

"Sergeant, do you think they'll need us now? Can't imagine the assholes won't surrender, maybe we can all go back home, don't seem they'll need our help to invade," another remarked.

"Maybe that's the good that'll come of it, we'll see," AJ replied.

Three days later, a second bomb was dropped, with equal devastation, and general elation broke out throughout the country. Going forward, an unending debate would commence and never end among the people all over the world of whether the bombing was good or evil. As for Sewell, he told his congregation that Satan had been unleashed, and all should pray for protection from the unending evil they would face ahead.

Six days later, the Japanese did surrender; the war was officially over, and this brought an early release from service to AJ and many others, and a few weeks later, he would pack, say his good-byes, and board the Greyhound bus for the trip home. He would surprise them by arriving home a full week before expected, and would purposely not tell.

Chapter Fourteen
Back Home

The Greyhound bus followed its tedious route down the narrow roads, around the curves, up the hills, and down the other sides, and the driver busied himself switching from one gear to the next.

AJ had, after some shuffling, finally selected a seat near the front, moved to the window side seat, and hardly looked up when a thin young man, also in uniform, sat down across the aisle and to the rear. Glancing to the side, AJ noticed his fellow passenger was blankly staring ahead, out the front window, and seemingly in deep thought. Finally, after the bus had gotten underway, AJ turned, and looking to the rear, broke the silence.

"Going home, soldier?" he asked as he looked over his headrest.

"Sure wish I were," was the short reply.

"Are you from around these parts?" AJ asked, noting sadness in the first reply.

"Once was," he answered.

AJ, sensing from his short responses that the soldier didn't want to talk, decided against further attempts, and from his forward seat, alternated looking at the upcoming road and the landscape passing by the side window. The bus labored forward up the steep inclines and picked up speed as it coasted over the crests while all the time the passing sights were becoming more familiar.

AJ wondered about the soldier's silence and speculated that he might be in deep thought about some trauma experienced, or perhaps about some unhappiness awaiting him at home. For some reason, AJ felt the need to reach out in comfort, but the opportunity did not present itself.

Two duffel bags, containing personal items from the army, rested in the rack overhead and AJ's eyes went to them frequently. When he looked at them he smiled, as a little child might harboring a pleasant secret, as he thought about the contents of one of the bags where he had carefully placed presents for his mother, Kathryn, and a special surprise for Melissa. He occupied his mind with thoughts about how he might present the gifts but nothing seemed appropriate, so he decided to wait and hope for the right time to reveal itself to him.

As he studied the passing scenes, he wondered what it would like be to be home for good since his life had changed so much. Where would he fit in, and would he reestablish himself in the family circle? These thoughts troubled him and he remembered his short visit a few months ago when he had felt uneasy with the changes occurring in his absence, changes he was unable to exactly describe. Had he been left behind, or was it that others had not changed at all, but that *he* had become different?

He had rested his forehead on the window, just as the long vehicle rolled over a cavity in the blacktop, jarring his head against the window pane, and his reverie ended. Refocusing on the scene up ahead, he realized he was now only a few miles from home and he soon saw the familiar post office up ahead. It was starting to get dark, and only a few people were still on the square, mostly those who were closing up businesses which had been active a few hours earlier on this busy Saturday.

The bus now pulled up to the curb and AJ rose and hurried to pull his bags down the steps, and for an instant the fellow soldier, from the rear, looked up with teary eyes into AJ's, quietly saying, "Take care, friend." By now, AJ was standing on the curb.

He was startled and speechless because in that instant he had the strange feeling that he knew the other soldier, so much so that he almost yelled for the bus to wait, but the driver had returned to his seat and was closing the door. The familiar whoosh sounded from air releasing the brakes, and the bus slowly pulled from the curb, leaving behind the odor of its diesel fuel.

AJ would never tell anyone about his strange encounter, that the feeling of familiarity with the stranger had overwhelmed him, but only for a fleeting moment. Secretly he thought that he had experienced a ghostly encounter with Billy Mullins, but of course he could tell no one, and this thought both upset and astounded him. The bus lumbered forward and he strained to get a last look at the soldier, but he was not to be seen, and he turned and saw a familiar figure approaching him.

Old Joseph Clark was the first to see him get off the bus. Joe lived just outside the town limits and usually was among the first and the last to be seen almost every day on the square, sometimes serving on the forum panel, other times working on his current whittling project. He cherished the opportunities the gatherings there gave him to socialize.

"That you, Aaron Joseph, Aaron Joseph Garrett?" the old man asked as he leaned forward on his cane and squinted his eyes for a closer look.

"Yes, it's me, Joe," AJ replied, adding, "It's good to see you, and how have you been?" AJ was still pondering the encounter with the soldier on the bus.

"Why, been just been fine, boy." AJ noticed the ever-present tobacco juice in the corners of Joe's mouth, and he thought, *Well, some things never change.* "I'm glad to see you back, we worried about you boys, Sarah expecting you're here?"

"Thought I'd just surprise her," AJ answered, "reckon anyone heading out our way soon? These bags are pretty heavy."

"Over there, that pickup belongs to the Stevens boy, he clerks at the hardware and should be leaving soon, he'll be heading out your way, let me help you carry your things over to his truck." Joe dragged his bag over but had to wait for AJ to heave both of them into the bed of the prewar vehicle. They waited for the truck's owner to return.

In a short time the young Stevens boy appeared and seemed anxious for the opportunity to give AJ the lift,

"Going right by there, do every day, sometimes see your folks out, bet they'll be glad you're back, heard a lot of talk 'bout you, understand you were some kind of policeman in the army. Heard you and Melissa Sullivan may be marrying, Melissa's my third cousin, I think, or something, you know." The young man hardly took a breath between sentences.

"Didn't know she had more kin around here, well, I was something like that in the army," AJ answered, smiling and wondering where the misinformation had originated, "just glad to be back and have it over with."

They pulled into the lane leading back to the old farmhouse and slowly came to a stop where the mowed grass designated the edge of the front yard. The headlights played on the front of the dwelling, and alerted Sarah and Lindsey someone was approaching, and they came outside to investigate.

AJ stepped from the truck, walked over and embraced his near faint mother, who kissed him several times on the cheek and kept repeating, "Thank God, thank God, for bringing my little boy back. Oh, Aaron Joseph, I missed you, and I'm so glad you're back, I haven't been at peace since you left, worrying 'n all. Lissie'll be so glad to see you, let's go inside, I want to be the one to call her and tell her you're here."

AJ shook Lindsey's hand and turned to the quiet, wide-eyed young lady staring at him from across the room, "Kate, is that you? I can't believe how much you've grown, you're not a child any longer, you're a beautiful young lady," and with that Kathryn came across the room and they hugged. Her shining knight had returned from the field of battle.

"Much obliged for giving me the ride," AJ said to the Stevens boy as he stepped off the porch and walked to his truck.

"You're welcome, and I'll be seeing you, folks, I drive by here pretty often." He ground the gears into reverse, and backed out of the lane and on to the road. In so doing, he passed a large tree, that Sarah, years before in her thoughtful mood, had named Aaron Joseph.

"Lissie, you won't believe, guess who's home, it's Aaron Joseph, little devil wanted to surprise us, you get ready, I'm a sending Lindsey to fetch you right now," Sarah had reached Lissie on the phone and the conversation abruptly ended with that short conversation.

Soon a bright-eyed and beautiful young lady hurried from Lindsey's car into the house, where the scene and the welcoming were repeated as the two embraced. It was a happy evening that only ended after someone remarked it was one a.m. AJ, having learned to drive, compliments of the US Army, drove Lissie home, where they sat and talked in the Sullivan lane an additional hour.

Several weeks passed before AJ commenced to feel more comfortable in his old surroundings. He spent much of the time visiting with neighbors and in town talking to old friends whom he had not seen in several years. He welcomed these encounters, as he felt uneasy when he was alone.

One day, alone, he went to the cemetery, and visited the graveside of his baby sister, Cordelia, and that of his father, Andrew, stood for a moment staring at their burial places, and then walked over to where they had buried Billy Mullins, and quietly spoke, "Hey, Billy, sure miss you, buddy, and wish you were here. Don't think I didn't recognize you on that bus; wish we could have talked awhile. Saw Martha a few months back, she's doing fine and your son looks a lot like you, but better looking. Want you to know that I'll watch over them, so rest well, my friend, be at peace now, Billie, me and lots of others loved you and will never forget you, I'll come back from time to time. By the way, you promised you'd put in a good word for me, don't forget that."

AJ was most at peace and feeling a sense of belonging when he and Melissa sat on the porch swing quietly talking, or when they took walks in the beautiful fall evenings. Once he turned to her and said, "You know, Lissie, I don't care much for fall. Everything seems to die; I'd rather prefer spring when everything seems to be coming back to life. Do you think that spring is God's way of showing us that there's something afterwards, I mean that death don't end it all?"

"I think so, AJ, never thought of it that way though," Melissa replied.

"Lissie, I'm troubled about something. Would you mind if I went away for a few days? There's something I feel I have to do down in Alabama, I want to see if I can find the folks of someone, it's sort of hard for me to explain," AJ asked.

"No, 'course I don't care, but hate for you to be away, you just got back," she replied.

"I won't be long, reckon when I get back, be here to stay then," AJ added.

She didn't push for further explanation, and he took her home.

AJ explained to Sarah about his proposed trip, was reassured that Lindsey's car would stand the journey, and the next day he started heading south, taking him over ten hours to complete the four hundred miles over the narrow two-lane roads.

Upon reaching Montgomery, and becoming hungry, he stopped at a small truck stop, noting a number of trucks in the lot. He remembered someone telling him this was a good way to gauge the quality of the food inside, and upon entering, he observed drivers laughing and joking with one another as they hurriedly drank the strong black coffee and consumed burgers and pie.

Seated, he asked his waitress if she could give him directions to find someone in the city. "I'm from out of town and don't know my way 'round, I'm from up in Tennessee."

"Ain't been here long myself, mister," she spoke, continuing to chew her gum, "but if I was trying to find someone, guess I'd go to the post office and ask, reckon they know everybody from delivering mail, you going to be around here awhile?" She smiled, probably hinting, and was obviously proud of the advice she had given.

"Just a couple days," AJ answered. "And where's the post office?" he asked, realizing how uninformed he must seem.

"Well, I do know that, get my mail there, here's what you do, you go on down this road about two miles, turn at the, let's see, one, two, three, third stoplight, Phillips 66 gas station on the corner, and turn left, it'll take you into town 'n the post office's just 'fore you get to the town square, it's easy to find," she replied.

"I'm much obliged," he said. He finished his coffee,

returned to his car, and headed down the highway counting stoplights, until he spotted the Phillips 66 station, then turned left.

He felt relief and was proud when the big building appeared, for he had successfully navigated his first big-city streets in an automobile. He parked the car and entered the building.

"Can I help you, honey?" the elderly clerk inquired.

"Yes, ma'am, I'm not from these parts and I'm trying to find somebody, they live in Montgomery, but I don't know where," AJ replied.

"Who you looking for, honey?" she asked.

"Last name's Farmer, they live out somewheres out in the country I think, a black family."

"Let's see here." She looked in a nearby book and ran her finger down a list. "F A R M E R, here it is, here's some Farmers, they all seem to live out on the Salina route, pretty rough area, about ten miles out this way," she said, pointing to a route map and giving detailed directions on how to get there. She drew the directions on a small piece of paper and handed it to him.

"I'm obliged, ma'am," and he started to leave.

As he exited, she smiled and added, "Welcome, honey, now you be careful driving, you hear."

AJ had never seen such a totally impoverished countryside, not in Tennessee, not in the Carolinas, and not in Europe, although certain run-down dwellings did remind him a little of North Africa. People sitting on their porches waved as he passed, and their children looked up from play in their dusty front yards and were seen retreating to the porches, apparently seeking refuge with the elders.

He turned down one dirt road to a certain crossroads, turned right, and carefully watched for a lane leading back from the road past a large weather-beaten barn feeling this must be the place circled on the small piece of paper.

A pitiful structure was just behind the barn, and like that structure, it was unpainted and the wainscoting was missing in places on both structures. On one end of the porch there hung a water bucket with a dipper hanging by a wire, a coat hanger fashioned into an improvised hanger. AJ had seen this sight before, but not for a long while.

One end of the porch was sagging and on the other end a support was bowing from the weight overhead. AJ speculated that only a little nudge would be necessary to topple the whole roof on anyone unfortunate enough to be below.

Some chickens were meandering on and off the porch as AJ pulled up, but when he parked the car, they cackled and scattered into the yard as he approached, and a red rooster tilted its head, eyeing him menacingly as he drew closer. Around the house it was quiet; no one seemed to be around, and in a distant tree, on a barren limb, a crow spotted him and cawed a warning to others that were busy foraging on the ground.

Glancing to the rear, he saw the remains of a harvested cotton crop in a small plot, probably no more than two acres, and on some of the stubble, little white tufts of cotton remained that had apparently been missed during the harvest. Just beyond and to the left, another small plot revealed the cut stalks where tobacco had been cut.

His eyes went to a rusty plow, its wooden shaft cracked, leaning on the side of the barn as though looking for some support from the leaning structure.

"Hello," he called out, "anybody home?" There was no response, so he called again, and stepped onto the porch, being careful to negotiate some loose planks.

A third time and an answer came from somewhere within the house. "We a coming, we a coming," and a gray-haired elderly man appeared, followed closely behind by a matronly and heavyset turban-headed black woman. She had a friendly face with a warm smile, and AJ's eyes fixed on her beautiful white teeth. Could it be that he was looking at Lemuel Farmer's mother?

"You wantin' us for some kind of business?" the old man asked, he turned and nudged his wife to the front.

"Just looking for some people, sir, I'm Aaron Joseph Garrett, sir. Was told the Farmer family lived out here, made a lot of turns and could be mixed up, you folks the Farmers?" he asked.

"I'm 'zekiel Fahrmer, wife here, her name Mary Ann Fahrmer, can we be of some help?" he asked, studying the tall young man standing before him.

"Well, sir, I'm really looking for the momma and papa of Lemuel Farmer, was Lemuel your son?" AJ asked, watching closely for their response.

Ezekiel's eyes widened and Mary Ann beat him to answer, "Oh my Savior, you know our boy Lemuel?" With the response her arms raised and AJ observed the palms of her rounded hands and the pleading look on her face.

"I just got home from the army, well, Lemuel and me, we were at the same places, we were both selected to be

in the Rangers. Was with him at a place called Anzio…"
AJ stopped.

"Lord, Lord, Lord, you knew our boy, can you tell us
about Lemuel when he was…hurt, oh my, bless you for a
coming to us, the others, they didn't know anything, just
said he had passed, and we wondered about it all. Do you
know how…how he passed?" she begged.

"Your son was a good soldier, yes, I was with him, but
we were all scared and running to avoid… There was
enemy all around us and the fighting was mean and
heavy, I just want you to know that Lemuel died saving
another man's life… He died a hero, he put himself in
front and got shot, and the other soldier, he was from
Chicago, he cried over Lemuel, and when things settled
down, we prayed for him. Lemuel was a hero and
everyone liked him a lot, and I wanted you to know how
he died. He didn't seem to suffer, just went to sleep, and
everyone knew that he had acted a hero." AJ finally got it
all out and noticed Ezekiel's nodding head as the old man
cried.

Mary Ann embraced her husband and looked at AJ
and spoke between sobs, "We loved our boy so much, he
the only child, oh Lord, we miss him plenty, we wanted
him to come back to the farm, seems all he wanted to do
was help his people live better with whites. Guess he did
all he could, I'm sorry we acting this way in front of you,"
she looked up with apologetic eyes, "we already cried
our eyes out."

AJ stepped forward and hugged her and then the old
man, he turned, and stared out at the car, "Reckon I have
to go now; I live a long way up in Tennessee, told my
folks to expect me back by the morrow. Here, take this,

I've written my name and address on this here piece of paper, you write me if you need my help," then slowly he walked toward the car and took a last look at the helpless old couple.

As he drove the country roads, he wondered if Lemuel had walked them as a youngster, and did he have friends, perhaps some young admiring girl who would never know the details of his passing. He thought, here was how the war had affected just one little family, and how the world didn't seem to really care, and about how this scene was likely multiplied a thousand times. *Maybe it's over and done with,* he hoped, *maybe people will now live in peace.*

Back on the main highway he pulled into a Texaco station with its familiar round sign and big star in the center, and while the owner pumped gas into the car, AJ got a cold Coca-Cola from the icy tub, picked up a moon pie to nibble on as he drove, and returned to the road that would ultimately lead him home. He felt good about this trip, relieved that he had done something he needed to do, and he hoped that when he got home this time, he would feel more at ease.

Chapter Fifteen
The Wedding

Kathryn spotted him first and ran out to meet AJ when he pulled into the lane and approached the house. As she waved, AJ was again impressed with how the little girl had grown up in so short a time. Four years ago she was just a little girl, but now, here was a beautiful young lady whom he hardly recognized.

At dinner, he told Sarah and Lindsey about his visit with the Farmers, how sad the encounter was, and how impoverished the area where they lived seemed. They were pitiful, he described, and how he wished he could have helped them.

"I thought our land 'round here was rough," he remarked, "but theirs seems totally spent, reckon they've never heard of rotating crops, folks there sure could use some help," he added.

That evening, when all the chores had been done, and they had eaten supper, AJ briefly left the table and returned from the back bedroom, where he had removed the three gifts from the duffel bag. He gave little silver-colored boxes to Sarah and Kathryn and both appeared totally surprised.

"My world, what have you done," Sarah exclaimed as she fondled the small box, but making no immediate attempt to open it.

"A present," Kathryn asked and added, "for me?" With childlike enthusiasm she pulled from the little box a delicate chain with a cross dangling from it. "Oh my," she held the necklace up to show Sarah, "I'll always treasure this, it's beautiful."

Now Sarah opened her box and removed another necklace, and hanging from its chain was a golden heart that opened up.

"Here, let me show you," AJ said as he took the heart in his hands and gently pried it open. "See here," he pointed out that there was an engraved message inside and returned it to Sarah, who studied the small print, and with watery eyes read it to the others, *To Momma, Love Always, Aaron Joseph.*

"I'm going to take this one over to Lissie, fetch her and be back soon," AJ said as he pulled another small box from his pocket after receiving hugs from Kathryn and his mother. "Reckon you probably know what's in here," he remarked with a sheepish smile, and he left the room.

Melissa got into the car, and before she could get situated, AJ thrust the small box before her and said, "This was awhile in coming, hope it suits you," and Melissa took it from him. She opened the box and removed the contents, a smaller, velvet-covered box, and with trembling hands she lifted its lid and commenced to cry. The beautiful ring was her first piece of jewelry, and it was all the more treasured because it came from her future husband. She worn it into the house and blushed as she showed the ring to Sarah, Lindsey and Kathryn, who made over it and hugged their future daughter and sister in law.

The wedding was not a large affair. Brother Sewell spoke his piece with predictable eloquence in addressing the bride and groom and the small gathering. The immediate families were there, so were a few neighbors and assorted elderly couples from the congregation. The Skaggs family, whom AJ had known all his life, were there, and so were Martha and her new husband, and that's how the gathering would be remembered, just family and close friends.

AJ stared at the beautiful and radiant Melissa, Melissa, now his wife; she stood beside him in her simple white dress that a neighbor had created for her, Melissa, with her beautiful coal-black hair, pretty smile, and a naturally beautiful face that shunned cosmetics. She was his!

Following Sarah's suggestion and an offer for the use of Lindsey's car, they honeymooned in Gatlinburg, that was, for Melissa, her greatest distance away from home since her trip to Fort Bragg. They walked the trails and saw their first live bear, rode across an enormous gorge in a swaying cable car, giving Lissie an upset stomach lasting for hours, paid twenty-five cents to have their picture taken with an enterprising Native American, and did countless other things that would be long remembered.

They would live with Sarah and Lindsey until their new house was finished. Their new home would sit on a high point up the road from the old farmhouse, and the view from its front porch took in miles of the surrounding countryside. Looking in one direction they could see an inlet of the lake, the portion that jutted in and covered the old Garrett farm, and looking in another direction AJ could point out Potato Hill, Abernathy Ridge, Kingsley Mountain, and numerous other recognizable geographic landmarks. The views were breathtaking from their two-storied dwelling, a home featuring indoors plumbing, and a network of electrical wiring. AJ and Lindsey helped build it and took pride in pointing out the home's modern features to others who stopped by to view the progress.

The year 1945 was a year of dramatic change for AJ and Melissa and those they held dear, and one that ended with hope and renewal.

-§-

Chapter Sixteen
The Seer

Sally McDermott was now approximately eighty-two years old, she had lost her husband, Obed, many years before and had modestly sustained herself out in Frog Hollow by collecting, from secret places in the woods, herbal remedy plants such a ginseng and snakeroot and an assortment of other cure-all plants respected by locals.

She was also the originator of her special remedy, concocted with much secrecy at the back of her property, known by locals to have as its base ingredient corn. When describing the product, a teller would usually cast a knowing wink at the listener, and remark, "I think you know what I mean." This product was reportedly of excellent quality, was known to greatly relieve pain and suffering, and had even achieved acceptability among many churchgoers. It provided Sally a nice income supplement and no one dared challenge this endeavor due to her poor circumstances, which, if made worse, would only draw more money from the county's near-depleted poor fund.

Sally was also considered by some to have a dark side and as being somewhat odd and strange acting at times. Area pranksters singled her out, almost always on Halloween, naming her the resident witch, and answering a dare, mischievous youths would approach her house on dark nights to warily peek though the windows. They would later exaggerate what they saw; "Crazy Sally" in the darkened front room, just sitting and rocking in a large chair, and seemingly doing nothing save stroking her big yellow cat resting on her lap. Such observances were told and retold to others, always growing and taking on new meanings, and poor Sally was soon pegged as a scary person to avoid, unless, of course, an herb or her remedy was badly needed.

And if that reputation was not enough, she was also known to practice some activities, denounced by the church crowd, among which was fortune-telling and palm reading, a skill she reportedly acquired after being kicked in the head by a horse when a little girl. It was not too uncommon to find ladies visiting her, on the pretense of checking her well-being, and making inquiry as to their upcoming fortunes. So it was that Melissa and Martha decided to pay her a visit one Saturday afternoon after baking a batch of sugar cookies for poor Sally. They would tidy up her house and assist her in a weekly bath and hopefully brighten the day of this ageing and fragile old lady.

"Hello," Melissa called, "Sally, you in there?"

"Yes, I'm right in here," was the reply, slightly louder than the noise from something she had dropped to the floor in the kitchen.

"It's Melissa Garrett and her friend Martha, we've come to see you for a while, and we're a coming in if that's okay."

"Why yes, you all come in, wasn't expecting company or I'd cleaned up a bit, who you say it is?" the old woman squinted and strained to recognize the two, "why, land sakes, 'course I know you two, you both sit down and let old Sally get you some water."

"Uh, no thanks, Sally, we're not thirsty," Martha replied, and the two cast knowing looks at each other, and Melissa raised her eyebrows. Not saying a word, they both knew what the other was thinking, that only in the most extreme circumstances would they ever put one of Sally's glasses to their lips.

"Sally, we don't mean to offend, but we've the afternoon on our hands, thought you might could use a little help tidying up, and maybe you'd let us to help you with your bath, we know it's a little hard for you to get around," Melissa offered.

"Well, I cleaned a bit this morning, but guess a little more won't hurt, and I haven't had my bath today, that's be nice," Sally said with a childlike expression. Both Martha and Melissa knew that the place hadn't seen a broom in weeks, and Lord only knew the last time Sally had bathed...but a mild odor gave hint that it hadn't been recent.

Their work started in the kitchen, every dish and pan was washed, the table was scoured and then the floor was swept and scrubbed with a powerful solution of lye soap and water. They moved into the bedroom, stripped the bed, and carried the foul-smelling linens to the outside, where they doused them in another tub of the strong solution and hung them over the fence to dry. Finally the front room got its turn and the house began to smell clean and fresh. They then helped Sally to the kitchen, assisted her in disrobing, and while Martha wiped down the frail body, her clothing was washed by Melissa. Five hours had passed, and now they looked at the poor soul and saw a contented face, a clean body, and glanced around the house and saw orderliness and cleanliness. They knew their labor was appreciated and worthwhile.

Now they all sat around the kitchen table and presented Sally with a sugar cookie and watched the delight on the old woman's face as she sampled it. They had found very little food in the house and nothing resembling a treat such as cake or cookie, and they resolved to report this situation to the congregation tomorrow. In the future, the women's auxiliary must routinely shoulder what they did today.

"Sally, you had any of your dreams lately?" Martha asked.

"Oh, child, old Sally dreams every night, 'times I get so scared with what I see, I worry for everybody, 'course I won't be here... Girls, I'm a telling you, there's troubled waters up ahead, great trials and tribulations, God's Son is a finally coming back." She took on a distant look on her face.

"When might that happen?" Melissa asked.

"Oh, it'll be awhile yet, lotsa change 'fore that, old Sally's seen it all, but I won't be seeing much more, be with Him soon, and be with my Obed again." She paused and sighed, "You know what I dreamed of the other day? Fell asleep right in that rocker over there, broad daylight, well, anyways," she paused again, "do you know they're gonna be able to put a new heart in a person when their old one gives out, I dreamed that, and I saw bigheaded men a walking on the moon, that's strange, but it's sure gonna happen, 'nother thing I saw, whites and blacks fittin' here in these parts, saw that, they's gonna be another president kilt, but I seen something I don't understand, they's two mountains, side by side, two buzzards were flying around and each one settled on a mountain, those big mountains, they just melted to the ground. Lordy, sometimes I break out in a cold sweat from my dreams, they scare me so. I don't mean to upset you girls though with my talking." Acting somewhat dazed and perspiring, Sally now seemed to return to the present.

Melissa saw her opportunity, "Sally, I don't understand those things either, but can I ask you something else, sorta wondering, will I have children?"

"Girl, I see you having two chiles, and the babies of both you girls will do just fine, they'll live out their lives...iffen they don't have accidents, but I feel sorry for *their* littleluns, end of time a coming 'fore their lives end." Now the old lady seemed to tire, and was noticed to lower her head as if trying to nod off, so the girls made sure she had something to eat and headed home.

"Don't you wonder how she comes up with all that, don't reckon she's talked to outsiders for weeks, no paper and no radio and all... It's just scary, do you really reckon our grandchildren will see the end-times?"

Martha remarked with some concern and then added, "And can you imagine, bigheaded people walking on the moon, glory!"

"It is fearful," Melissa replied, thoughtfully adding, "What if she turned out to be one of those prophets, there were lots of them in the Bible, whatever, I'm worried about her, we've got to get the women at church involved in helping her."

That evening the Garrett family was just finishing supper and remained seated around the table talking about the weather, crop rotation, and the quality of the bread pudding as well as numerous other subjects which solicited polite interest. Melissa related that she and Martha had visited Sally McDermott the day before. "Found her in great need, pitiful conditions around her house, and she didn't seem to be caring for herself... We told several at church this morning and I guess somebody's making up a schedule for people to go tend her, won't be long till someone's going to show up and find her dead. Poor thing, she's still mentally sharp though. She got to talking about her dreams and told us she'd seen bigheaded people walking on the moon and went on and on about a bunch of other things...said I'd be having a house plumb full of kids," she said, as she turned and looked at AJ for his reaction.

"Walking on the moon," AJ said as he looked up from his serious work of lathering another piece of cornbread with butter, "well, you know it could happen, the Germans, they used a rocket bomb against England, thing streaked all the way from Germany to England, reckon they could make it stronger, and shoot it all the way to the moon." Then he thoughtfully added, "Odd about Sally's talk, she must have picked up on that somewhere. Whoa, just a minute; did you say a house plumb full of kids? Think I'll just be on one of those rockets and head for the moon," and they all laughed at his response.

Within six months, Sally passed away and was laid to rest next to her beloved Obed at the church cemetery. In future years, others would recall certain things she had spoken of, and eyebrows would be raised as her predictions unfolded. It made them wonder if the end-times were really this close at hand.

-§-

Chapter Seventeen
Twigs

The local paper heralded it just as they always did for every birth, marriage, death, vacation, relocations, visitations, accidents, big-ticket purchases, and church gathering of any sort:

Jacob Andrew Garrett was born September 23, 1946, and the 8-pound baby boy and mother Melissa are doing fine. Aaron Joseph Garrett is the proud father and the grandmother is Sarah Garrett Stone. All live in the Mahalia's Crossing area.

Somewhere else in the paper there was less important news of the first United Nations meeting and another story told of a recent Winston Churchill speech in which he described something understood by only a few, that there was dropping down across Europe a dividing line between the Soviet Union and the Western world, something Churchill called an "Iron Curtain."

Lately, discussions on the town square included matters involving happenings throughout the nation and even remote places overseas, places and people that had been mentioned by those returning from the war, and events being described in the nightly radio news broadcasts.

Some new retail outlets now occupied the town square, a restaurant, with its flashing neon light *Bird's Café* sign, fast becoming the place for morning coffee and dissemination of news, and a new farm implement store displaying items unavailable during the war years. Commerce, like everything else, seemed to be picking up steam as the local populace enjoyed the benefits of higher incomes and the monies funneled back from the big cities. But there were a few things that remained unchanged.

The benches in front of the courthouse were still there with the absence of grass underneath due to their constant use. The ageing Basil Strode was still there, weather permitting, preferring the benches, where he could easily dispose of his tobacco juice. People got so accustomed to seeing him in a certain spot that his absence always drew concern about his well-being.

And over at the Garrett farm, AJ and Lindsey, tired but pleased with their day's work of picking corn from their most productive fifteen-acre field, collected their gear and headed back to the barn. Working together, the two completed the job in one day, a job that would have taken them at least a week just five years ago. After being dried and readied for the market, the corn they picked would bring a high price, as had been the case with the wheat and alfalfa previously harvested. The Garrett family prospered and during the oncoming winter they would further extend their land holdings.

Having left Lindsey at the barn, AJ walked down the road and up the path to their new home, a colonial-style two-story that he and Lindsey had completed over the past year. As he approached, he couldn't help but wonder how in the world he would repay the bank loan that made the building possible; after all, its guarded price was over eight thousand dollars! *Why, we didn't pay that much for the whole farm,* he thought. Maybe it would all work out, things were definitely looking up and he admitted he felt pride when passersby, pointing to the structure, would remark, "That's the new Garrett place." The house increased his feeling of belonging; something that was diminished while he was away. Now he had a place.

Sarah and Kathryn were there helping Melissa with the baby by washing what seemed like an unending number of diapers. *Thank goodness for the new electric Maytag washer with the wringer,* she thought, remembering what a problem the diapers used to be. Back then, she only had a few, cut from an old sheet, so she had to handwash them often. And in the backroom, Jacob Andrew Garrett was exercising his lungs with a high-pitched cry, hopefully for food and not for reasons of colic. If he sensed that he had been born in the lap of relative luxury, he was not expressing appreciation.

"Aaron Joseph, where's Lindsey?" Sarah asked, as he entered the room.

"Left him down at the barn, he was going to the house and get cleaned up, said he'd come up here after that," AJ replied.

"That's good, me and Melissa fixed supper here this afternoon, we'll start putting it on the table while you wash up, but first see if you can make that child of yours hush up. His crying going to make us all go crazy," Sarah said.

Some time passed, still no Lindsey, so Sarah asked, "Kate, would you go fetch your daddy, and tell him if he don't come soon, he's going to miss his supper."

"I'll go get him," Kate replied, and the thirteen year-old hurriedly left the room out the side door.

Shortly thereafter, Lindsey came in through the front door and laughed at the situation of having missed his daughter who minutes earlier had left through a different door.

"Like one of those Charlie Chaplan movies," he remarked, "by the way, did anyone from that car come up to the house?"

"What car, Lindsey?" Sarah asked.

"The car that was in the lane, I saw it pull in there when I was going to the house from the barn. Looked like the driver was lost or having car trouble, leastways, he was driving awful slow," Lindsey remarked.

"Weren't no one at our door, and I didn't notice the car. Now do you suppose you or Aaron Joseph could get Kate back in here so we can sit down for supper? If we don't get at it, the food's going to get cold and won't be fit to eat," Sarah offered.

AJ immediately left and strode down the road toward

the old house, but en route and arriving there, saw no signs of Kathryn, and he yelled toward the barn, "KATE, everyone's waiting on you, are you at the barn? Kathryn, where are you?"

There was no reply, nor any sign of Kate at the house nor the barn and not along the way.

Thinking she had perhaps doubled back to their house and was now with the others, adding to the humorous chain of events, AJ returned but was dumbfounded to discover that Kathryn was not among them.

"Went to the house and the barn, Kate was not there, where could she have gone so quickly?" he said as he looked to the others for a possible answer.

"Lindsey, you go one way, Aaron Joseph, out the other way, both of you go down to the road and trace the way to the house, she might have fallen on the way and be hurt, it's cold out there and it's getting dark, so hurry," she urged.

They both walked down the long drive and to the road, then on to the house, fully expecting to find her sitting somewhere along the way with an ankle sprain, or distracted by some form of wildlife on her journey. But she was nowhere to be found and they were now becoming alarmed.

So the supper was put on hold and Sarah, Lindsey and AJ, leaving Melissa with the baby, quickly exited and once again walked the route while calling for her facing different directions. Still no Kate, and the time that had lapsed would not have allowed her to get beyond the sound of their calls.

On the way back, and nearing the point where the lane

to the house met the road, now in partial darkness, Sarah, who was a little ahead of the others, spotted something white lying on the side of the road.

"Look! Here's Kathryn's handkerchief, she *did* come this way," she called out. The two ran up to her side.

She then looked about scouring the immediate area more closely. "What's that over there, it's a shoe, here's one of Kate's shoes, what in the world is happening here, my Lord, Lindsey, where is she, this isn't like her at all, something bad has happened."

"That car," Lindsey blurted out, "that car that pulled up into the lane, do you suppose... My God, AJ, run down and get the car, I'm going to call Sheriff Mitchell."

As recent as five years ago only one twelve-phone party system extended beyond the center of town, and this was a system that fortunate neighbors had strung together for use in emergencies. On that system there existed an intricate number of rings code designating a social call or a call for help. Now, however, almost every house along the highway had phone service, and anyone connected could simply tell Marjorie Smith, the central switchboard operator, whom they wished to call and she would efficiently ring the house or the place of business. Improved communications was perhaps one of the greatest changes that had taken place in the community.

"Marge, ring Lenny Mitchell at home please, this is Lindsey Stone," he asked.

"You sound upset, Lindsey, someone sick or something, how's Sarah?" She often entered into such conversations with callers but no one publicly complained.

"We can't locate Kathryn, Marge, just ring Lenny if you will," Lindsey replied. Five rapid rings brought about the connection, with strong suspicions that Marge remained on the line.

"Lenny, Lindsey Stone, we got a problem out here we don't understand, my daughter Kathryn left Aaron Joseph's house about an hour ago going down the road to our place and we can't find her, we've been out looking and calling but she's gone somewheres. We fear something's happened. Suppose you could come out?" Lindsey asked.

"I'll call some others and be there in a few minutes," the sheriff replied.

Shortly, Lenny, and three others arrived and they joined in the search after a short briefing. With flashlights in hand they all took to the darkened area outside, retraced the immediate area, and then commenced to venture into the nearby woods. An hour later they returned but had found no traces of the little girl. While their search continued Sarah updated Marge, who, in turn, generally spread the alert throughout the community.

Because no one had ever faced a missing person problem before, they were generally befuddled as to what they should do, so they decided to assemble at the sheriff's office and draw up a plan of action. At daylight, a group scoured the land surrounding the Stone-Garrett properties once again, and Sheriff Mitchell notified surrounding authorities of the situation, something he called an APB, and with Lindsey and AJ, the three headed north up the highway to neighboring communities. They would stop occasionally and ask if anyone had seen anything unusual the night before and specifically had anyone seen a large black sedan vehicle. North seemed the logical route as Lindsey remembered the strange car was heading north when he saw it pull from the Garrett lane.

At the start of the day little else was talked about in town except the missing Kathryn, and by noon, it was likely that everyone in the county had heard details of the mystery. The phone rang almost constantly at the Stone and Garrett houses and people stopped by offering help and speculations as to what may have happened.

There were many theories, but the most prominent one, although only whispered one to another, was that Kathryn might have eloped to Alabama since her age qualified her for marriage there, but for obvious reasons, no one dared share this theory with Lindsey or Sarah, knowing the hurt it would cause, and out of regard for the unpredictable reaction it could bring. Word circulated that Lindsey was not easy to deal with in his increasing emotionalism.

"If someone took my little girl and hurt her, I'll kill them, I'll kill them right on the spot," he was heard to remark, and, much to Lenny's concern, Lindsey had placed a long-barreled Colt revolver under the front seat of his car. Sarah tactfully cautioned him not to use it, no matter what, but she understood his feelings and secretly felt the same.

Just after noon a call was relayed to Lenny from the sheriff of Batesville, a little town in southern Kentucky. The local sheriff there reported that the owner of a general store had called and reported that a car had awakened him late the night before, and had purchased four gallons of high test. The driver had also bought some candy and some cheese and crackers, and of all strange things to be purchased at eleven thirty in the evening, a pair of sandals! He remarked the man had a problem getting together the money to pay for the stuff.

No, there was no woman, but the man said his little girl needed to use the toilet, and reported she was sick in her stomach. The owner told him the restroom was out back and the man went part way to the back with her and, at the time, he thought that strange although he reasoned it was dark back there.

The call left no question about the sighting and within an hour the local sheriff, AJ, Lindsey, and Lenny, with his flashing emergency light placed on his car's roof, sped to the general store and confronted the owner.

"Did you see the girl?" a tense Lindsey immediately asked as they entered the store and even before they were introduced.

"No, not up close, just noticed she was a youngster, I was writing up the sale when they passed that side of the building," the owner replied, pointing in the direction of the restroom.

"Did she seem hurt?" Lindsey went on.

"Didn't see her up close, but she was able to walk, I know that," he replied.

"Did you get a good look at the car?" Lenny then asked.

"Well, I think it was a four-door, it was black and didn't look too cared for, like maybe it'd never been washed," the owner offered.

"Tell us about the man," AJ inquired. "Big? Fat? How was he dressed? And did he say anything about where he was heading?"

"Men, I'm sorry, but I was sort of sleepy to begin with, and the only thing really unusual was someone buying gas that time of night, he might have been a little scruffy, and he didn't say much of anything, now I know you need my help, but that's all I saw," he apologetically said, and then added, "Know one thing, four gallons of gas wouldn't get him very far."

The four looked at each other not knowing what else to ask, and they told the owner they might be back, and if he remembered anything more to call, and with that they commenced to leave the store. Walking toward their car, they thanked the sheriff and decided to proceed to the next town, some twenty miles further, hoping that something more would be discovered. But before getting in their cars Lindsey excused himself, indicating he had to use the restroom before they left.

Back in the little room Lindsey was looking at the graffiti-filled walls and something caught his eye, something that may have been freshly scratched on the soft pine wood and he studied it more closely. He looked down and noticed a nail lying on the floor, and then saw that the scratches spelled out *E-town, K*.

He summoned the others back and showed it to them. Yes, it was recently scratched on the wall, but what did it mean?

"My God," AJ exclaimed, "*Elizabethtown, Kathryn!*"

They speculated, and then agreed that maybe it *was* possible, and hurried to the car. Elizabethtown was about a hundred miles further up the road and they decided to go there. Discussing the situation, they all agreed that the little girl was smart enough; and she was capable of doing such a thing. It wasn't much to go on, but it was all they had and it was encouraging.

Heading up the road, they stopped at a filling station in the little community of Creekside. The owner there had nothing to offer but said he'd be watchful, and then they proceeded to Harpers Junction, a little town twenty miles further. There, from the local sheriff, they heard something that prompted further questioning.

"I don't know a whole lot about it," he said, "but I run into the Coca-Cola driver earlier today at the café, he asked if I'd heard anything about the wreck just outside Jonesboro. Said a car had pulled off 'side the road and a lumber truck barreled into its rear end. Totaled the car. Guess there were two people taken to the Granger hospital. He wanted to know if I'd heard whether or not they lived."

"Did he say what kind of car?" Lenny asked, hoping for the right answer.

"No, he didn't, apparently man and wife was in the car. Lot of accidents in that section, the stretch is dangerous. People tend to drive too fast along there, lot of hills and dips in the road, no place to stop. Don't have many places to pull over when they get in trouble," he replied, adding, "Where you all heading?"

They explained who they were and their business, and, "Be much obliged if you'd keep an eye out for a black car containing a man and little girl."

Shortly after passing through Jonesboro they spotted the wreck scene that was made obvious by the remainder of a spent flare on the road, and over to the side in the ditch, there was a hub cap and a piece of black fender the wrecker had missed. They spent little time at the site and headed on to Granger.

They became more fearful of the outcome when they spotted a mangled black four-door sitting in a lot beside the Esso station just before entering Granger.

"Lindsey," AJ said, revealing concern in his voice, "I hope Kate wasn't in *that* car. I don't think anyone could have survived that mess. God help whoever was in it."

"Oh God, no, don't let it be my Kathryn, let's get to the hospital," was Lindsey's short and quiet response.

"Who are you?" the doctor asked. "Are you akin to the man and his daughter? We couldn't call anyone, there was no identification."

"You mean you don't know who they were; does that mean they were both killed in the accident?" Lenny asked.

"No, I'm sorry, the father was killed, the daughter suffered a pretty serious concussion, but she's going to be okay," the doctor explained.

Explaining the circumstances, Lenny asked, "Is it okay if we see the little girl? We might know who she is."

"Yes, down here," the doctor said, adding, "I'll go with you, but please don't excite her, be quiet, she's just coming out of a coma, and we don't like to shock or upset such a patient."

As they walked to the room Lenny further inquired, "Who was the man, any idea?"

"Well, our sheriff indicated there was nothing on his person but he found some items in the glove compartment. 'Course we can't be sure but we think the man might be someone from the St. Louis area. You might want to talk to the sheriff."

It was her, and Kathryn, although groggy, recognized Lindsey immediately and tried to rise but the doctor urged her to lie still. She commenced to weep but smiled when she saw AJ. She was safe and the physical and mental healing would begin, but it would be many years before she could function a single day without the memory.

"Daddy," she weakly spoke, "the man said God told him to take me, and he made me get in the car, we ran out of gas and he pulled to the side of the road... What happened to me?"

"Don't get upset, baby, did the man hurt you... I mean, did he do anything wrong to you?" Lindsey asked.

"No, Daddy, he didn't touch me. He said we were going to start a church, he kept rambling on real strange," she managed to haltingly explain before she closed her eyes, drifting into a calm sleep.

The sheriff later explained, "We're pretty sure who he is. Goes by the name of The Most Reverend Jeremiah — was involved with a religious sect over in the St. Louis area. Best we can put together, he was run out of town. He was a real con. Don't mean to make fun of a dead man but he, shall we say, he fleeced the flock and some oddball followers came looking for him, and he took off, the car belonged to a cult member. He has a pretty long police record."

A week later Sarah and Lindsey took their little girl home, where she gradually settled in and returned to school, her adjustment greatly aided by the presence of a smiling nephew who had overcome his bout with colic.

An October rainstorm surprised everyone one evening, unusual for that time of year, and the remaining leaves from trees rained down, setting the scene for the winter months. A healthy little offspring bid good-bye to its secure branch high in a tree, and just as the parent tree had done before, fluttered in the wind until it fell unnoticed, and next spring it would sprout and ensure a new generation.

Chapter Eighteen
Times of Transition

The postwar years between 1946 and 1951 brought about many changes, affecting not only the Stone and the Garrett families but also the community, the nation, and, for that matter, the entire world.

To begin with, improved communications caused the world to grow smaller and most everyone understood the implications of the Cold War and Churchill's Iron Curtain. A news item about the distant Berlin airlift could elicit firsthand knowledge from veterans who had been to Berlin, and offered the locals greater insight about the story. The relative glut of information brought with it a growing feeling of unrest that had been foreign to the community heretofore.

The courthouse square forum might just as likely hear talk about the pros and cons of the Marshall Plan in 1947 as they would Noah Cross's accident while harvesting his wheat, or that Jackie Robinson, a black man, was now allowed to play Major League baseball, as they would that Inez White had given birth to a baby girl.

For locals, shouldering the problems of the world was dealt with by simply applying solutions that had always worked on the local level, so as the complex issues rolled out, the editorializing, although sometimes simplistic, flowed forth:

1946 VERDICTS at NUREMBERG:
"They all ought to be hanged."
1947 MARSHALL PLAN:
"We spent money to tear 'em down, now we spend money to build 'em up, it just don't make sense."
1947 TRUMAN DOCTRINE:
"Old Harry, he'll set 'em straight."
1948 SOUTH AFRICA APARTHEID:
"If they can't get along, they shouldn't be together."
1948 STATE OF ISRAEL DECLARED:
"God said He'd bring 'em back. End-time's coming for sure."
1949 SOVIETS DETONATE A-BOMB:
"Stage being set for Armageddon."
1950 NORTH KOREA INVADES THE SOUTH:
"Surely to goodness, they won't get us involved in that mess."
1951 22nd AMENDMENT LIMITS PRESIDENCY TO TWO TERMS:
"Guess they're afraid we might give 'em another Franklin Roosevelt."
1951 H-BOMB:
"Stage being set for Armageddon."

Grist for the mill, and they ground it finely.

National items of interest usually focused on the industrial and technological developments, as these sectors vigorously awakened in the postwar years, and the oft-heard comment was, "Land sakes, what won't they think of next?" and this usually sufficed.

They heard and talked about an electronic computer, whatever that was, and that a man had built the largest airplane ever...and it flew, at least a short distance. They wondered what in the world he'd do with it now. Someone had invented a camera that developed its own pictures that probably would replace their Kodak box cameras. Someone else had flown around the entire world and a few television sets appeared on the local scene. The general population remembered the little four-inch screen set displayed in the hardware store window only a short time ago when they gathered on the sidewalk and watched, in black and white, *The Kukla, Fran and Ollie Puppet Show*. They found it hard to imagine that pictures might soon be in color.

New cars, on their way to an unknown destination, passed through town more frequently and one day a sleek 1951 Studebaker Champion stopped at the local gas station, where a few gathered to inspect it. The owner anxiously peered out the station window at them and became amused when he overheard someone remark, "I hear tell the government might take 'em off the road because oncoming cars can't tell whether they're a coming or a going."

It seemed every day something new and awe-inspiring was seen on the television screens or read about in the *Daily Chronicle*. The people generally wondered where all this might possibly end, and they debated whether this or that was a good or bad thing. "Reckon God meant it to be," seemed to settle more and more arguments.

The community was changing along with the nation and the world. Families, chasing a higher standard of living, left for the big cities, and many didn't return, and some others, reaching their seventies and eighties, passed away and took names with them etched in the area's history. The benches on the courthouse square were now empty, the grass under them filled in, nature erasing their tracks, and it seemed odd without Basil Strode and old Joe Clark sitting there talking, laughing and whittling. Both died in 1950, and there were several more missing whose names AJ had heard his entire life, names that were from the generation that made up the grandmas and grandpas.

By now almost every home had electricity and had been retrofitted with indoors plumbing except for a few exceptions, the power lines had not been strung to a few homes in Frog Hollow, and although available on the edge of the road out front, a few strong-willed residents rejected the current as being evil and opted out for the time being.

A few new families moved in but it would take time for them to be woven into the community fabric, and while they were not shunned, it was just that their roots were shallow and it would take a few seasons for them to take firm root.

And soon the word got out that the large expanse of water was filled with prize fish, and was excellent for boating. A new element began to show up particularly in the summer months and spawning new ways for the locals to make a living.

And at the Stone residence the daughter of one of the area's most prominent farmers, who had seized the opportunity to add relatively inexpensive farmland, won the local spelling bee and almost moved to the next level had it not been for misunderstanding the pronouncing of the word "CORNUCOPIA."

Ole Ring, AJ's dog, the last non-human vestige of life in the holler, died at age ninety-eight in human years, and was laid to rest where the yard ended and the woods commenced. And a little six-year-old boy increased his daily range of exploration, comprehending the finality of death, and was coming to understand and question the environment where he had been placed.

But the greatest blessing was bestowed upon the Garrett family in 1949, when Aaron Joseph, and Melissa Garrett, along with their son, Jacob, welcomed a daughter and little sister, Anna Marie Garrett. But unlike the birth of her firstborn, the birth of little Anna came after a lengthy time of labor and proved to be physically hard on Melissa. The doctor at the clinic cautioned her against having additional children, as it could prove fatal to the mother

When AJ came into the room to see his new daughter for the first time, he found a totally spent and weakened Lissie there waiting to greet him.

"Lissie, you look so tired, are you okay?" he asked as he came to her side and kissed her cheek.

"Tell the truth, I feel awful weak," she replied as she turned and pulled back the blanket which had been tucked around the baby's face. "We got us a pretty little girl, don't we?" Lissie said, and added, "She favors her daddy a little."

"Nah, not like me, I see a pretty mother in those eyes, she's going to be a fine-looking young lady," AJ said as he softly touched the infant's cheek with his index finger.

"AJ, do you remember what Sally said about our family, you know, that time Martha and me went over to clean for her?" Lissie asked.

"You mean about us having a house full of kids?" he replied.

"Well, I never told you different, but she really didn't say that, AJ, she said we'd have just two children, and I guess she was right, from what the doctor said."

"I love you, Lissie," he said, and they embraced.

After they took her home, it didn't take long until Anna was able to pull herself up and take her first steps and then she spent much of her time pestering her big brother, Jacob.

Seasons came and passed, they formed the years, and each changing cycle of death and renewal brought an equal share of goodness and disappointments to those in the fast-changing community.

But some yearned for the return of simpler times, and were never able to reconcile why, among countless other issues, their friend President Truman would yank McArthur out of Korea when our boys there were still in harm's way.

Chapter Nineteen
Jacob Goes to School

With the addition of two rooms, even the former one-room schoolhouse could not escape change so an expanded building awaited the latest group of first grade students. At least the building was familiar to most of the newcomers, because they had attended Sunday school in the building ever since they could remember, and had closely monitored the room additions since construction commenced.

"Good morning, everyone," the recent graduate of the local technical college said as she looked over the top of her wire-rimmed glasses and smiled at the twelve freshly scrubbed faces. They responded by eyeing her suspiciously, and no one returned the salutation.

"I'm Mrs. White, and I'm very proud to be your first grade schoolteacher," she continued while smiling, "and I'm going to work very hard to make school for you exciting and fun."

They continued to quietly size up this person, who was foreign to the community, noting that she looked friendly enough, and she did have a nice smile, but they'd have to wait and see. After all, they'd heard stories about some teachers, and the tales hadn't included much about fun and exciting learning experiences and also her being pretty and younger didn't seem to fit either. Something was just not right here, but in fairness, they'd give her a chance, as if they had a choice.

"I'm from Benton County and my husband and I own a small farm there and he also works for the Tennessee Valley Authority, he's one of the men you see putting up the telephone poles that bring electricity to us. Does everyone in class have electricity in their house?" she asked, surveying the group for a response.

This time a few nodded yes while others continued to stare and made her wonder if she was approaching them properly.

"Now I've introduced myself, I'd like to hear all about you, so one at a time, you tell me who you are and something about your family and anything else you'd like me to know about you. My, you all seem so quiet, young lady, why don't you go first," and she pointed to a pale, freckled-faced little girl in the front seat. "Stand up here please," and the little girl nervously rose and came forward with bowed head.

She stood for a moment, almost paralyzed with fear and speechless, then she looked about the room and blankly stared at her friends with whom, only an hour earlier; she had spoken freely as they had filed into the small classroom.

Mrs. White looked at the little girl and, glancing down, noticed a damp spot on the floor at the little girl's feet, and saw that a classmate had seen it and snickered, and the teacher remembered a similar incident involving her in the fifth grade when she attempted to explain a science experiment. Her words wouldn't come out then either, and she remembered how the blood had rushed to her own face, and how the quiet seconds seemed to be minutes of agonizing silence. The experience caused her to still have an aversion to public speaking.

"I think I know your name," Mrs. White said, as she gave her a compassionate look, "isn't it Alice White? Your last name is the same as mine, you know, we might be kin."

"Yesum," little Alice replied as she looked up from fixedly staring at the floor, nodded, and exhibited the hint of a smile.

"I understand you like to help your mother bake, and you're very good at making cookies. Is that so, Alice?"

"Yesum." Now tears welled in the little girl's eyes, she wanted badly to just blend in with the crowd.

"Maybe you'll fix some cookies and bring them to school, we'd all like that, wouldn't we, class?" this time addressing the others. They all nodded yes and warmed up to the introduction session. But across the room Theodore Stokes, the little boy who had snickered, was now mischievously smiling, and was seen to lean over and heard to whisper to a classmate, "She peed on the floor!" The fellow classmate quickly looked away from Theodore to avoid responding.

Picking up on this and understanding what was happening, Mrs. White menacingly glared at the two and the smiles disappeared as she said, "Now, Alice, that's very good, you may sit down, and let's ask some others to introduce themselves," and the little girl quickly moved back to her seat with an expression showing great relief.

"And who are you?" she asked, summoning the young man in the third seat. She noticed that the boy was a good two inches taller than the others and his thick brown hair, streaked from the sun's rays, caused him to even look taller. The teacher noticed his wide-set eyes and high cheekbones, but had no way of knowing these features were inherited from his mother, who, like all the Sullivan ancestors before her, had lots of hair and wide brown eyes. She had passed these traits on to her son, who now came forward with no apparent shyness.

"I'm Jacob, ma'am," he volunteered, very businesslike, and without further prompting.

"And does Jacob have a last name?" she asked, smiling.

"No, I don't think so, I'm a Garrett, ma'am," he offered, and the teacher marveled at the reply.

"Do you live near here?" she asked.

"Yes," he quickly replied. "We Garrett people have always lived here. My daddy and grandma, they came from down in the holler...but it's covered with water now. My daddy knows where it is, he's shown me where they lived, but like I said it's under water now. My grandma killed a snake that got in their house down there once. Daddy told me it scared 'em to death. I never knew Andrew, he was my grandpa; a tree fell on him and killed him before I was born. He's buried out back if you want to see his grave. He's buried next to my aunt; she died when she was a baby. My daddy says I look a lot like

170

my grandpa Andrew, Let's see, I got another aunt named Kate, and she's smart, she won the spelling bee. Her daddy is Lindsey, he's my second grandpa and he's real nice. And my momma's name is Melissa and some call her Lissie or Mrs. Garrett. And one more thing, I have a baby sister, and her name is Anna."

"And where do you live Jacob," she asked.

"Uuum, we live out in Mahalia's Crossing...on a farm, but everyone here already knows that, they already know me and I know them," he added with a thoughtful pause. "I already know my ABC's and I can count to five hundred."

"Well, that's all very good," added Mrs. White, "I think you're going to do just fine in school, now let's see who else we have in class. You may be seated."

"Yes, ma'am," and he walked to his seat wondering if he had missed anything.

In turn, the remaining ten of the first grade class came forward, introduced themselves, and Mrs. White recognized, even at this early time, that her greatest challenge might be to instill in Theodore Stokes some level of functionality in the basic scholastic skills.

The Stokes family had lived in Frog Hollow for years and the family had a long history, most of which could be reconstructed from reviewing the county welfare records. Their name in the community had become synonymous with the words "poor" and "lazy," and it was not uncommon for a father to warn a laggard son or daughter, "You'd better work harder or you'll end up like the Stokeses...or in the poorhouse," and this usually called up such a dire image the child would immediately be goaded into a higher level of effort.

The idealistic Mrs. White looked upon Theodore with unusual compassion and accepted the challenge of making something out of him. He seemed to fit nicely the description of the unknown who was described by the dean in his commencement address at the college. In that speech, he told the new graduates, and that included Mrs. White, "*You* can make a difference, to change just one life, so go forth and…" she couldn't remember the entire speech but she knew what he was trying to get across and was inspired by it.

Lord, give me the strength and wisdom to help this little boy, she thought, just after another student informed her that during recess, Theodore had eaten the tube of toothpaste which the Tennessee Board of Health had provided for passing out to all the students. While toothbrushes were not in common use, most knew to chew the end of a small sassafras branch and use it for brushing the teeth with the paste.

Not fully understood at the time, good fortune had truly rained down on Theodore Stokes when he encountered Mrs. White because she stuck with her goal to ultimately equip him with the basic education tools to earn a living and thereby raising his self-esteem. Theodore would one day prove his ability to function extraordinarily in a more complex environment, and while she had no way of knowing, the little unkempt urchin standing before her would one day own his own plumbing and electrical supply business. It served much of northeastern Tennessee.

June, the following year, soon came and Jacob completed his first school year and proudly presented Melissa with his grade card that showed grades in the upper nineties and a note from Mrs. White:

*Jacob was a pleasure to have in class, I feel he has
exceptional abilities and a strong desire to learn. He
ranks highly in citizenship. L. White*

Jacob had tucked his first report card in the pocket on
the bib of his overalls and started his mile walk home
anticipating the oncoming summer's excitement. He
passed the big oak tree on the right and noticed that a
squirrel had started to build a nest high in the top. He
heard the warning call of a crow and spotted it sitting in
the upper branch of a dead tree in the distance. He knew
it had selected a good watch-out position, giving
unobstructed vision of the ground below, where its kind
foraged. Surely the crow was aware that its black outline
could be easily seen, Jacob mused.

Was it too late to hunt the elusive "dry land fish?"
Probably so, but spring was late this year and he had
found a full sack of the delicious mushrooms only a short
distance from the house three weeks earlier. No, it'd
probably be too late to find any more; they were only
available for a few short weeks in the spring, but now
spring had passed. He remembered how the grownups
had made over that bounty, and his mother had even
stopped what she was doing, breaded and fried that
batch, and how they all enjoyed a few bites of the
delicious spring treat.

A truck, some distance away, was heard coming closer
and finally appeared just up ahead coming at him. It was
the bread truck heading to town and it finally reached
him, and then passed on by. The driver, he didn't know
his name but he knew him by sight, always waved when
passing. Jacob stopped for a moment and waved back as
the big vehicle went on its way.

Just beyond the edge of the road and across a cleared strip, where the tree line of the woods started, Jacob saw that the mayflowers were now at least a foot high, a sign that the summer months were approaching. And on the distant hillsides, the dogwoods had already lost their beautiful white flowers and soon a little red berry would appear. His daddy had shown him the way to hollow out a pithy branch from the tree and, with a smaller branch, propel the little berry through the improvised barrel at high speed toward a target. He remembered how they stung when they hit a person and that they shouldn't be aimed at an eye.

That reminded him; he needed to make himself a new slingshot as he had lost his old one. Hopefully he'd be able to find an old inner tube, because he'd need two strips of the rubber to make the sling. Finding the Y-shaped tree branch was easy, and an old shoe tongue was the perfect size to hold the stone, but it was hard to get your hands on an old inner tube, that is, one not too rotten. He thought this was going to be a great summer, and he had a lot to do to get ready for it.

Soon the house of his grandma came into view and then, a short distance further, there was his house, and he knew they would all be waiting for him. He patted his breast, to make sure the grade card was still secure, and quickened his pace and suddenly, up ahead, Ring, his dog that had replaced the former Ring, raced toward him at great speed. And after he had walked up the lane to the house with the tail-wagging dog, and climbed the steps to the porch, he found the most welcome sight, his mother, and she hugged him and kissed his cheek.

"Jacob, this is a very good card, what's this citizenship mean?" Lissie asked.

"Missus White says that's for minding my P's and Q's and getting along, I think Missus White wrote that on everybody's card," Jacob replied.

"Well, I'm glad you showed you wanted to learn," Lissie added, as she attempted to draw some reaction from him.

"Yesum, where's Daddy?" Jacob asked as he surveyed the area.

"Well, he was up at the north field, said he was going up there to hoe weeds, but he should be back by now, why don't you run up and get him?" Lissie asked.

Jacob found AJ sitting at the edge of the field, approached him, and announced, "Well, school's out for the summer, I got good grades, Momma said to ask you down, she's almost got supper ready. Are you done hoeing?"

"Done all the hoeing for today, want to leave *you* some." He smiled at Jacob and added, "What's that, you say you got good grades, well, I'd expect that from you, Jacob, someday you're going to grow up and be real smart and full of book learning, yes, sir, your daddy's going to be real proud of what you make of yourself."

AJ started gathering his tools and explained, "I was just resting here a minute, hoeing got me tired, reckon we should be going. Figured Lissie would be looking for me. Oh, hey, wait a minute; I got something here to celebrate you a doing good in school. Over there, see there, at the edge of that row, see that little tree. Why don't we take it up and plant it in front of the house, case we need some shade later."

And they took a generous amount of dirt from underneath, lifted the little foot-high tree from where it

175

had rooted, and carried it to the yard in front of the house. AJ looked down at Jacob and asked, "How's this spot here, Jacob?"

"Be a fine spot," Jacob replied, and they placed the little tree into the small hole they had dug, gently packed dirt around its roots, making sure it was upright, and walked toward the house.

Lissie, who had stepped out on the porch and having observed them kneeling, asked, "AJ, what were you and Jacob doing out front?"

"Oh, we just planted a tree, our Jacob got good grades at school," he replied, and, looking down at Jacob, he added, "We just planted a tree named Jacob."

-§-

Epilogue

A somewhat secluded little community in hilly eastern Tennessee remained insulated from outside influences for many years. Mainly this was probably because no one felt the area had any economic potential, except its locals, who took pride in their land ownership that had passed down many generations. Its residents farmed but mostly only growing crops to satisfy their personal needs. They did raise some cash by planting a little tobacco, and by harvesting the plentiful supply of readily available timber. But other than a few factories turning out inexpensive clothing, there was no industry. The area was not shunned; but for these reasons, it remained sheltered from the world beyond their vision.

Really, not much had happened in this remote part of the country, but to its credit, it had produced Cordell Hull, an acclaimed Secretary of State, and there was of course Alvin York, who had, according to local talk, almost defeated the German army singlehandedly in

World War I. By and all, however, the area remained secluded, and few visited except for special reason.

It was in this background that the independent Scotch/Irish Garrett family, living on a small bottomland farm, had survived for years taking great pride in being self-sufficient. They were God abiding, respectable, and mindful, above all else, that these legacies must be passed down from generation to generation.

Andrew had married Sarah and they were happy doing what others had done before them, farming and commencing to raise the next generation of Garretts, but then the first sadness entered their lives when their baby daughter died of pneumonia, becoming the first infant Garrett to be buried in the church cemetery. Then, Andrew had his fatal accident, leaving Sarah and her young son, Aaron Joseph, with meager means to survive, but they somehow did, despite great hardship in the years right after Andrew's death.

Everything commenced to change in the community when others from the outside world entered their lives. Water would come and fill all the lowlands after the Obey River was dammed up. This brought electricity, and a beautiful, expansive lake, but this good was at the expense of low area farms that were eliminated. The extensive construction project would bring others to the beautiful area, among them a newly widower husband for Sarah named Lindsey Stone, and his daughter, Kathryn, and this man would become a father figure for Aaron Joseph. But it also brought the changes that slowly transformed the area's culture, and only time would be able to judge whether these changes would be for the good or bad.

Aaron grew up, went off to war, and returned a hero of sorts. He married a beautiful local girl, Melissa, and they would leave two surviving children, Jacob and Anna. The Stone and Garrett families would acquire land, be blessed with success, and collectively become two of the state's well-known families.

Their prominence grew beyond the state in the late sixties when Aaron Joseph came to the aid of a black family in Montgomery, Alabama, the parents of Lemuel Farmer, a comrade of Aaron, who had been killed during the war. The ageing couple was being harassed by Klanners, who had first burned a cross in front of their humble dwelling, and then set fire to their barn. Federal agents were investigating the incident, and on national television, Aaron was seen accompanying the subjects to meet with FBI agents at the courthouse. After justice had been served, a followup account, again commanding national attention, witnessed Aaron Joseph's return to their farm with a barn-raising group of volunteers from his home community.

Little Kathryn, Lindsey's very bright daughter, grew up, graduated with honors from the University of Tennessee, and taught school in Cookeville for several years before returning to the area to assume the role of principal at the local high school. She was helpful in editing a book written by her stepbrother.

William "Tooch" Mullins's son grew up and became a successful home developer, capitalizing on skyrocketing land prices, and building countless resort-type dwellings for the horde of summer residents now migrating from surrounding states. Along the way to his success, Jacob's father, Aaron Joseph, mentored the Mullins boy over the years, and Jacob looked upon Tooch's son as an adopted cousin.

Anna married a young man who would work his way up the political ladder and become a member of the state legislature, and Jacob, in addition to farming, would also become a respected area attorney.

The community's early pillar of faith, Pastor Sewell, in what the flock hoped was a weak moment, accepted the devil's invitation and backslid, and caused more than a few to marvel at the extent of his fall from grace. He left the area in shame after a husband returned home early from the day's work discovering the pastor's hat lying on the bed and the bedroom window open, and a wife begging for forgiveness. The pastor, apparently forgiven for his own sin, reemerged several years later achieving popularity as a healing evangelist on national television, and locals never missed a program.

Sarah and Lindsey both passed away in the seventies, and Aaron Joseph and Melissa Garrett were laid to rest near them in the church cemetery in the late nineties, leaving only Anna and Jacob to carry on the family name. Hundreds of people, some not locally known, attended each of their burials, and at the interment of AJ, a military color guard gave him a gun salute and taps were played in the distance, adding to the sadness of the event.

Only Jacob would remember being told by his mother the prediction made by Sally McDermott about the two mountains and the buzzards and see the relationship to the World Trade Towers when they crashed to earth. And he often wondered if he would live long enough to witness her end-time prediction, but reasoned it really didn't matter.

And throughout all these human journeys, two beautiful maple trees grew and prospered, and witnessed the changes affecting the humankind, one out by the road in front of the Ledbetter-Stone property and the other in front of the home of Jacob A. Garrett.

The lives of the humans would expire with certain earthly finality, but the trees would seem to die, yet again emerge in the spring of the new year, giving hope to those wise enough to understand.

When I look at those trees my eyes sometimes fill with tears recalling the people and events that transpired since they were seeds ordained to survive by a never-ending power, and I proudly remember that one tree is named "Aaron Joseph," and the other "Jacob."

Jacob Andrew Garrett

CPSIA information can be obtained at www.ICGtesting.com
Printed in the USA
BVOW01s1223171214

379811BV00001B/32/P